Working as a high-profile lawyer for his shifter pod, Saul Davison keeps prying eyes away from his wealthy Alpha Kaiser Rush's affairs. His position earns him wealth and prestige due to being a cutthroat in the courtroom. The fact that he's secretly a lion's mane jellyfish and won't settle down for anyone but his mate, earns him the reputation of a playboy. Saul enjoys both — the finer things the money buys, as well as the plethora of floozies attracted to his bed.

When Saul finds himself repeatedly returning to a small coffee shop, he can't understand the allure. He doesn't even like coffee. Sitting at a table, drinking chai tea, Saul is pondering the oddity when a young Hispanic human approaches him . . . and asks if he can join Saul. Saul's knee-jerk reaction is to say no, but there's just something so earnest and sweet in the human's expression — not something that normally attracts him. Buying time, Saul offers his hand.

As the human slides his palm against Saul's — introducing himself as Mateo — a zing of awareness rushes through Saul's body, and it all becomes clear. Mateo is his mate.

Can Saul win his sweet young human's heart and share the world of shifters with him, or will his reputation get in the way?

Jetboating with a Jellyfish
Copyright © 2023 Charlie Richards
ISBN: 978-1-4874-3939-2
Cover art by Angela Waters

Published by eXtasy Books Inc

Look for us online at:
www.eXtasybooks.com

Jetboating with a Jellyfish Beneath Aquatica's Waves 15

By

Charlie Richards

DEDICATION

Push yourself, because no one else is going to do it for you.
~Unknown

CHAPTER ONE

"Your hottie is back."

Looking up from the dishes he was washing, Mateo Barrera stared at Tina. The barista was smirking at him, her blue eyes dancing with mischief.

"He ordered hot chai tea again," Tina continued with a roll of her eyes. "Why does he come to a coffee shop every day and order tea?"

"Not everyone likes coffee," Mateo murmured as he thought about the tall slender hottie who'd caught his eye the prior week. "Or maybe he doesn't do a lot of caffeine in the afternoons." Mateo didn't know why, but he felt the need to defend the handsome man's choices. "And he's not *my* hottie."

No matter how much I'd love for it to be true.

Ten days before—*yes, I'm counting*—Mateo had exited the back to bus the tables. He had just been finishing up the final table when the man had walked in. Mateo had frozen, the cloth he was using to wipe the table resting on the top, as he watched the stunningly distinguished man cross to the order counter.

The stranger was tall—Mateo guessed he stood around six-and-a-half-feet tall—with a whipcord lean body covered in a suit so high-end that Mateo couldn't even guess at the designer. With his pale blond hair slicked back from his face and reaching his shoulders, he showed off his aristocratic features. The man's pale blue eyes reminded him of shards of ice that sent the best kind of chill down Mateo's spine.

1

In a word, Mateo thought the man was stunning.

A customer crossing in front of Mateo's line of sight had caused him to jolt, and he'd quickly rushed into the back.

After that, Mateo had snuck a peek into the front area every chance he could. He'd discovered that the suited man visited every afternoon between one and one-thirty. He would order a hot chai tea, drink it at a table near the door, and then leave.

On Tuesday, Mateo's day off, he'd almost gone to work just to sit with a coffee during that time so he could see him. In the end, he'd known that would be weird. He'd stayed home with his fantasies and right hand.

"So, you gonna put on your big boy manties and go see him?" Tina asked, poking Mateo in the arm to get his attention again. "I know you haven't taken your break yet."

Mateo felt his cheeks heat just at the idea of walking out there and approaching the handsome blond. Except, as he nibbled his bottom lip, he wondered if he could do it. The image of him holding the man's hand across the table popped into his head, sending a warm churn through his gut.

Why the hell couldn't I do it?

After all, Mateo didn't have anything to lose. Even if the man turned him down, he could still dream about him and lust after him. That wasn't any different than what he was doing now.

Jerking a nod, Mateo muttered, "Okay. I'm gonna do it."

Tina whooped softly, clapping her hands. "Go get 'em, tiger." Grinning, she grabbed the dish towel off the counter and used it to whip his butt. "He's all yours."

Mateo rolled his eyes as he used another towel to dry his hands. Still, he couldn't help but smile. He really did appreciate Tina's acceptance.

Far more than I ever got from my own family.

As soon as Mateo had come out, his family had disowned him. He'd figured they wouldn't be pleased, but to completely cut him out of their lives? Mateo hadn't expected that.

I just thought I'd have to deal with some disapproving looks or guilt-driven religious talks or something.

Except, that hadn't happened.

After all, like many Hispanic families, Mateo's family were devout Catholics.

When Mateo's mother had asked him when he was going to bring home a good girl and settle down like his brothers — he had two older brothers as well as two older sisters, all married and three of them with kids of their own — he hadn't been able to lie anymore. He'd told the truth. It would never happen because he was gay.

Mateo's father had narrowed his eyes and demanded, "Don't you disrespect your mother that way."

When Mateo had apologized while insisting he was telling the truth, his father hadn't said another word. He'd risen to his feet, taking his sniffling mother with him. Then he'd turned his back on him, using his hold to force his mother to do the same.

Frozen in shock, Mateo had watched as one by one, his siblings and their spouses had also risen. They'd frowned at him, shaking their heads. Then they'd gathered their kids and left for another room.

Mateo hadn't known what else to do but leave. As he'd left the house, the sound of his mother crying had just about ripped out his heart. He'd tried calling her the next day, but she hadn't answered. When he'd attempted the day after, Mateo had nearly had his heart broken all over again when his father answered the phone, told him never to call again, and that he was having Mateo's number blocked from all their phones.

He'd spent the day moping around his apartment in his pajamas, alternating between crying and eating ice cream while cuddling with the battered stuffed cat his mom had given him when he was four — Pace.

Fortunately, Mateo's buddy, Lee, had arrived and helped

him through his funk.

Pushing thoughts of his family away, Mateo took a deep breath. He headed to the break room and took off his apron. Then he returned to the front. Seeing the handsome distinguished blond sitting at the table by the front window, Mateo paused, his courage faltering.

"You can do it," Tina whispered into his ear, giving his arm an encouraging squeeze.

Mateo nodded as an idea formed.

Heading behind the counter, Mateo began to prepare an iced chai tea latte.

Maybe he hasn't tried it iced before.

Saul Davison sat in the coffee shop, sipping his chai tea and wondering what the hell he was doing there.

I don't even like coffee, and the smell in here is . . . cloying.

That was why Saul always sat near the door. Every time someone entered or exited, he would get a bit of fresh air. Which brought Saul back to his confusion.

Why do I feel compelled to keep coming back here?

Ten days before, Saul had met Detective Grisham Canton at the place. It was close to the human's precinct, and he'd wanted to collaborate with him regarding a couple of cases. Grisham was mated with Cuzco, a coconut octopus shifter who was part of their shifter pod.

The second Saul had walked in, the lion's mane jellyfish he shared his psyche with had perked up in his mind. Normally, while on land, his other half lay fairly dormant—a quiet presence within him. As Saul had moved to the counter to order his tea, that had changed.

For some reason, his jellyfish began to trill in his mind. Saul had been tempted to walk around to try to ease his animal's sudden curiosity, but Grisham had arrived. After discussing a couple of possible problems that would take Saul's skill as the pod's lawyer, he'd discreetly explored the place. Saul had even found a way to stick his head in the back, but he couldn't figure out what was bothering his jellyfish.

Saul had spent a couple of restless nights before giving in and returning. He sat with a tea every day and people watched. After all, the thought had occurred on the second sleepless evening that perhaps he'd scented his mate in one of the customers.

With that idea in mind, Saul sitting beside the door had a second purpose. He could scent each person as they came in and out. Except, after coming back so often, Saul was beginning to second guess himself.

Saul took the last sip of his chai tea. As he swallowed, he stared into the mug, debating getting a second cup. Except, Saul knew he had a lot of research to complete.

Shifting his weight, Saul prepared to stand. Movement to his right caught his attention, making him pause. He spotted a Hispanic male heading toward him with a pair of cups in his hands.

The fact that the guy's dark-brown eyes were pinned on him and he had a pensive expression on his face gave Saul pause, and he relaxed back in his seat.

"Hi," the man greeted softly, stopping beside the table. "Um, I noticed you always come in and get hot chai tea." The man was clearly nervous, shifting his slightly plump body from foot to foot. Holding out one of the cups, he offered, "I-I thought you might like to try the iced chai version."

"That's very thoughtful of you," Saul began slowly, surprise filling him. He couldn't remember the last time he'd been openly flirted with outside of a club. As Saul reached for the drink, he admitted, "I've not tried that, yet."

In truth, Saul preferred hot drinks, but he didn't mention that to the male. He didn't want to insult him. Saul couldn't imagine how much effort it took the Hispanic-looking,

slightly overweight male to approach someone like himself—
a white guy in a high-profile suit.

While Saul didn't have a racist bone in his body, he knew
there were certain facts of life. This man screamed nerves, and
his clothes were clearly department store variety. They
draped over his frame, hiding his curves.

Too bad. I bet the curves are adorable.

Huh. Weird thought.

Especially since when Saul went to a club, he was never
attracted by shyness or denim-covered curves.

"Um, I-I hope you like it," the man stuttered when Saul
took the drink. "Um, I'm Mateo. D-Do you mind if I, uh, j-join
you?"

After taking the cup from the man, Saul did his best to ignore the ever-so-slight tingle that traveled across his fingers
when they touched. Despite the way the hairs on his forearm
stood on end, he racked his brain for a polite way to decline.
Saul didn't want to hurt the man's feelings, after all.

Saul opened his mouth just as the jingle of the bell heralded
the door opening. A customer walked in accompanied by a
swirl of fresh air. In the next instant, Saul's senses were
flooded with the most amazing aroma—sweet and masculine,
with a hint of soap—and it was coming from the Hispanic human who'd brought him a drink.

Well, hot damn.

He's my mate.

No wonder my jellyfish kept drawing me back here.

Lifting his free hand, Saul indicated the seat directly to his
right—as opposed to the one across from him—at the small
table. "Thank you for the drink, Mateo," he murmured, just
managing to keep his growl of anticipation from his voice.
"And I'd love for you to join me."

Saul saw Mateo smile, and it created a flutter in his belly
that he'd never before experienced. The way a strand of
Mateo's black hair separated from the rest, laying across his

forehead, caused Saul's fingers to twitch. He very much wanted to brush it from his forehead and tuck it back with the others.

Damn. I'm a controlled, dominant, high-powered lawyer. What the hell?

"Um, thank you," Mateo murmured, sliding into the seat. His smile appeared shy. "Uh, so, you get tea here?" With his cheeks taking on a pleasing pink hue, Mateo softly asked, "Not an afternoon coffee drinker?"

"I don't like coffee," Saul answered honestly. After all, this was his fated mate—the one man he could bond with and twine his soul with—and the one person he should always be honest with. His shifter nature would always demand no less. "I enjoy tea far more." Seeing Mateo's surprised look, Saul allowed him to process that by taking a sip of the iced drink. The pleasant flavors of chai tea burst across his tongue while cooling his throat when he swallowed. "Oh." Saul snapped his attention to Mateo. "That's really good." With a soft chuckle, he muttered with a shake of his head, "Why haven't I tried this before?"

Saul could see himself enjoying the drink often on a hot summer day. Spotting Mateo's pleased smile, Saul grinned larger than he recalled . . . ever. He liked that look on his soon-to-be lover's face.

Gods, finally. Finally, I'll never have to search for companionship again. I'll always have it.

With a shy smile, Mateo shrugged. "I don't know." He cleared his throat as he shifted in his seat before wrapping both his hands around his own mug—coffee, from the scent of it. "Um, are you against iced drinks, too?"

Chuckling softly, Saul shook his head. "Not really. Just, uh—"

Saul paused.

How could he explain that Saul had researched images for powerful lawyers and they seemed to go hand in hand with either coffee, bourbon, or golf.

Weird human shit, and I don't want any of them.

Saul preferred wine.

"When I think of cold tea, I always think of the sweet tea popular in the south, and I'm not a fan," Saul admitted with a soft scoff. "What about you? Are you a regular here?"

If Mateo was, it would explain why Saul's jellyfish had sensed his presence while he'd missed his scent.

To Saul's surprise, Mateo shook his head. Then, upon his next words, everything made sense.

"No, I work here." Mateo's cheeks darkened a little bit more. "Uh, I'm a dishwasher here, and I bus tables."

Saul nodded, understanding. If Mateo bussed tables, then he would occasionally travel through the room. That meant his scent would have been spread around the place. While Saul hadn't noticed it because he tried not to inhale too deeply, his jellyfish obviously had.

"Do you enjoy your work?" Saul asked curiously, wondering how difficult it would be to separate Mateo from his job. He would prefer having the man in his home at *World of Aquatica*, and a forty-five-minute drive for a dishwashing position wouldn't be pragmatic, in his opinion. Seeing Mateo's brows shoot up, Saul chuckled as he continued, "Or is it just a job?"

Mateo cleared his throat as he glanced over his shoulder. "Uh." When he returned his attention to Saul, he muttered, "It's a job. Pays the bills."

"What's your passion?" Saul rested an elbow on the table, leaning toward the much shorter human. He really would like to be closer so he could enjoy his scent more.

"Uhhh, well—" Mateo began, his brows furrowing. "I suppose—"

"Oh my god, Saul!" A perky voice interrupted Mateo. "I thought that was you." A second later, a lithe blond pressed

against Saul's arm. The man even went so far as to begin trac-
ing his fingers through Saul's hair as he cooed, "I've been
waiting for your call, handsome." Giving him a heated look,
he lowered his voice. "I'd love another night with . . . you."

Saul felt a muscle tick in his jaw as he leaned away from
the touchy-feely male while batting away his hand. Seeing the
pout that immediately turned down the man's full, lip-gloss-
covered lips, a vague memory surfaced. He recalled picking
up the human in a club.

"I, uh, I better get back to work," Mateo mumbled, jumping
to his feet. "Glad you like the tea."

Before Saul could call after Mateo — or extricate himself
from the clingy vine that had appeared — the cute human hustled into the back.

"Wanna buy me a drink?" the blond asked, batting his eye-
lashes after plopping into Mateo's vacated chair.

Pinning a cold look on his one-night stand, Saul replied
bluntly, "No."

*Just great. I meet my mate and get interrupted by a past fuck.
How the hell do I fix this?*

Exiting the coffee shop, Saul ignored the blond's call in favor of pulling out his phone.

I need some advice.

CHAPTER TWO

M ateo had never felt so mortified in his life. His short conversation with the handsome man couldn't have made
it plainer that he would never be someone the walking wet-
dream was interested in. He hadn't even introduced himself.

The hot stranger had asked if he liked his job, which
seemed polite. Except, what if his boss had overheard Mateo's
admission that, essentially, it was just a paycheck? Talk about
uncomfortable. Then the man had asked if he had any passions.

The guy obviously wondered if I had any aspirations beyond me-
nial, blue-collared work. I wonder what he would have said if I'd
admitted to picking up seashells as a passion. Or whale-watching.
And that I never want to go to college.

Mateo just wanted to make enough money to keep a roof
over his head, food in his belly, and have a little cash left over
to enjoy the occasional fun.

To top it off, one of the man's past conquests had shown
up. It had only proven what Mateo should have already figured. There was no way he was the sexy man's type. Their
differences couldn't have been more blatant.

The man who'd pressed against the hottie—a guy who'd
obviously been intimate with him—had been lithe and mus-
cular. He'd had short, spiky-blond hair and vibrant blue eyes.
The guy had even sported eyeliner and lip gloss—maybe
even a little blush.

Mateo, on the other hand, he was Hispanic, through and
through. He had the traditional black hair, medium tanned

10

skin, and dark brown eyes. While he had a bit of muscle definition, because he'd never been sedentary in his life, he loved his burritos and empanadas just a little too much, and it showed around his midsection — to be precise, the little extra weight on his belly and hips.

Mateo and the little hottie that'd damn near plastered himself to the tall slender sexy man's side couldn't have been more different.

God, what was I thinking?

At least I'll still have my fantasies.

Just as Mateo had reminded himself before going over there, nothing had changed. He could still fantasize about the man. In his dreams, Mateo could give the handsome man any personality he wanted.

Well, I guess there's one change.

Mateo had to admit that truth, at least to himself.

I no longer have hope of someday being with the man.

With a shake of his head, Mateo returned to work. He found the simple action of washing, drying, and putting away dishes soothing. It gave him something to focus on other than his disappointment.

"Hey," Tina murmured, bumping his hip with her own as she passed him. "I saw what happened."

Mateo glanced Tina's way, but he didn't bother responding.

"Don't let that hussy get you down," Tina told him. "I still think you have a shot at him." She carried her apron in one hand, telling Mateo that she must have been finished with her shift. "As soon as you left and that other guy sat down, he totally bolted, leaving that hussy interloper in the dust."

Forcing down the niggle of hope that Tina's words gave him, Mateo shook his head. "Naw, I doubt anything would have come of it," he told her. He couldn't totally hide his disappointment when he smiled at her. "He's so far out of my league. I don't know what I was thinking."

Tina smiled warmly. "Opposites attract?"

Mateo scoffed. "That's only real in books and movies."

"Well, if he comes again tomorrow, I think you should try again," Tina declared with a decisive-looking nod. "He liked the iced chai you took him. I saw his look of surprised pleasure."

"Yeah," Mateo confirmed softly. "Yeah, he did."

"That's something, then," Tina pointed out. "He'll definitely remember you." Tapping his bicep, she optimistically stated, "Maybe he'll want to buy you a drink to return the favor."

Yeah, right.

"I doubt—"

"Tina, stop interrupting Mateo at work." Marshal, one of the managers of the place, stopped beside them. The man was usually a pretty laid-back guy, and he didn't mind them chatting with each other. Still, Mateo knew they were at work, and Marshal's next words reminded him of that. "The tables need to be bussed, Mateo."

"Yes, sir," Mateo immediately replied, grabbing a towel to dry his hands. "I'll get right on it." As he hung up the towel, he smiled at Tina. "I'll think about it. Thanks, Tina." As an afterthought, Mateo added, "Have a great night."

As Tina responded with, "Night," Mateo turned and grabbed a blue tub and started toward the front.

"Think about what?" Marshal asked, falling into step with Mateo. With a chuckle, he pressed, "What's Tina trying to talk you into?"

"I took a drink to a customer that I'm attracted to," Mateo admitted softly, pushing through the swinging door. He kept it vague, uncertain if Marshal knew he was gay or if he would care. "There didn't seem to be a spark, but Tina thinks I should try again."

"Oh, yeah?" Marshal smiled, surprising Mateo by asking,

"Which guy caught your fancy?" The manager must have noticed his shock, for he chuckled softly as he told him, "Yes, I know you're gay. No, I don't have an issue with it." Marshal shrugged. "You're a good worker. Always on time and you do your job. I don't care what you do in your bedroom."

"Wish more people felt that way," Mateo muttered before he could censor himself, thinking of his family.

"Someone hassling you about your sexuality?" Marshal sobered, his voice quiet. "Who? This is a no harassment establishment."

"Oh, no." Mateo shook his head. When he saw that Marshal didn't look convinced, he stated simply, "My family."

"Aww, damn, man," Marshal murmured, grimacing. "Sorry to hear that." Then he patted Mateo on the shoulder before saying, "Good luck with the guy," before walking away.

Mateo refocused on work.

The afternoon flew by, keeping Mateo busy. While his thoughts occasionally drifted to the hottie, he managed to keep himself distracted. At the end of his shift, Mateo removed his apron and shoved it in his bag before placing the strap over his shoulder. He needed to take it home to be washed.

Grabbing his jacket, Mateo slung that over his arm. He headed toward the back door. While he'd needed the extra layer on his walk into work that morning, he knew the weather would have warmed up to a comfortable level for a walk in his short-sleeved button-down.

When Mateo walked out the door, he immediately turned left. He started around the building, heading for the alley that would take him to the sidewalk. When Mateo heard his name called in a silky tenor, he was certain he was hearing things.

13

"Mateo," the man called again. "Please, wait. Can we talk?"

Mateo turned and just managed to keep from gaping. The tall, sexy man from the coffee shop was striding toward him. His long, suit-clad legs were eating up the ground between them in an enticingly predatory gait that caused Mateo's heart to beat faster and his blood to heat in his veins.

"Mateo?"

The sound of his name on the man's tongue was making it hard to think of anything but how he longed to hear this man say it in the throes of passion.

Focus, damn it. He already thinks I'm an idiot.

"Uh, hello, sir." Mateo decided to go with the polite approach. "Um, can I help you in some way?"

Like suck your cock?

Shit! Focus on something other than sex.

To Mateo's surprise, the man's sigh sounded disappointed. "You don't need to call me, sir, Mateo." Then his thin lips curved into a slight smirk. "Well, not unless you're into that, but we'll discuss that later." Before Mateo could even process that insinuation, the man sobered and told him, "First off, I came to apologize. And secondly, I'd like to take you to dinner." For just a second, he seemed to hesitate before he added, "I'd like to get to know you, Mateo."

"Y-You do?" Mateo could hardly believe it. "Why?"

The sexy man scoffed softly, surprising Mateo by lifting his hand and gently skimming the backs of his forefingers down his jaw. The soft touch caused him to gasp as he stared up at the man. Mateo had to tip his head way back to meet the guy's gaze. Just as he'd suspected, he stood six-foot-six, and Mateo thought it would feel so nice to be tucked within this tall man's arms.

"Because I'm attracted to you, Mateo," came the man's shocking response.

"You are?"

The man's smile appeared sensual as he rested his hand on Mateo's shoulder. Mateo felt the man rub his thumb along the side of his neck, causing the hairs on his arms to stand on end. His breath caught in his throat as warmth flowed down his chest, and his nipples beaded. That heat hit his belly, then his groin, and he barely swallowed his moan as his dick quickly filled.

"Yes," the hot stranger declared. "Will you let me take you to dinner this evening?" The man lifted his other arm and checked his watch—a *Rolex*, and Mateo would bet it wasn't a knock-off. "Let's say, five-thirty. Will that give you enough time to get ready?"

"Yes," Mateo replied breathlessly.

The man grinned, showing off even white teeth. "Excellent." Keeping his hand on Mateo's shoulder, he pulled out his phone and used his thumb to wake the device. "What's your address?"

"I-I don't even know your name." Mateo blurted out the words, and his cheeks flushed hot as embarrassment filled him.

Damn. Now he'll think I'm an idiot for sure.

Shit. I don't need a one-night stand screwing up my potential mating. I seem to be doing a bang-up job all on my own.

Grimacing, Saul offered, "I'm so sorry." He forced himself to release Mateo's shoulder. The smooth skin of his neck had just been too enticing—along with the burning desire to touch his mate. Holding out his hand, Saul stated, "My name is Saul Davison, and it's an absolute pleasure to meet you, Mateo."

When Mateo slid his palm against Saul's own, taking his hand, a tingle worked up his arm, and goose bumps rose on his flesh, hidden by his suit jacket.

Just damn. Can't wait to experience what it'll be like for all my mate's naked flesh to move against my own.

Saul's cock throbbed with his desire, and he felt grateful that the jacket was long enough to hide his groin.

"Nice to meet you," Mateo replied.

While his human's voice sounded soft, shy even, Saul could smell his mate's arousal. The delicious aroma surrounded him, making his own need soar. His balls felt heavy, and he felt a bead of pre-cum escape him.

Holy shit. I need this human so fucking bad.

The desire to get Mateo to the nearest flat surface began riding Saul hard. Except, he knew he needed to be a gentleman. Mateo wasn't just some fuck. He was the other half of his soul, and Saul needed to treat him as such.

"So, your address?" Saul pressed, needing to move things along before he gave in and took him to his SUV's back seat. *Wait, my SUV.* "Or I could give you a ride home."

Mateo hesitated, and Saul figured his human would say no. To his pleasant surprise, after a second of nibbling his plump bottom lip, Mateo nodded.

"Okay," Mateo replied quietly. "Um, thank you."

Saul squeezed Mateo's hand—mentally reveling in the knowledge that he'd never tried to pull away after the handshake—before releasing him. He immediately moved his hand to Mateo's lower back. With a gently push, Saul guided his mate forward.

"It's in a parking garage to the right," Saul shared, putting his phone away so he could point in that direction. Then another thought occurred to him, "Or did you drive to work?"

"No, I walked," Mateo confirmed. Then he quietly added, "Even if I hadn't, I'd just come back for my car later."

Mateo muttered his second comment so softly, Saul wondered if he'd heard him correctly. Then he scented the slightly peppery scent of embarrassment, and he realized that he had. Saul decided to let it go, pretending he hadn't heard.

"Good," Saul stated, glancing down at his much shorter mate. He guessed Mateo stood five-foot-nine. With Mateo's thicker body, Saul knew he would be perfect to hold tight in his arms, pressing against his own. "Got any favorite foods I can help you indulge in?" Another thought occurred to him. "Or allergies to stay away from?"

"Um, I'm allergic to shellfish," Mateo told him. Then he wrinkled his nose. "Um, don't really care for fish, either. Tried a fish taco once, and that was just nasty."

Saul couldn't help his soft chuckle. "No seafood. Got it." He wondered what Mateo would do when he revealed that he could turn into a lion's mane jellyfish—one of the largest species. The fact that his mate didn't eat marine life amused him, considering Saul lived in a pod of shifters made up of those kinds of animals. "I'd be happy to give up fish for you."

Mateo snapped his attention to him, surprise on his features. "Oh, you don't have to do that," he countered with a shake of his head. "Just because I don't like it doesn't mean you can't eat it."

"Hmmm," Saul hummed. Turning them into the parking garage, he began leading them to his SUV. "And if I were to eat fish, the flavor of it on my tongue . . ." Reaching the SUV, Saul couldn't resist turning his heady-smelling human. He put the smaller man's back to the SUV's side and eased close to him. "Would you want to kiss me?"

"K-Kiss you?"

Saul relished the breathy catch in Mateo's voice. Seeing the way he panted, his chest drawing in heaving gasps, he felt his control begin to slip. When Mateo swiped his tongue over his bottom lip, the move drew Saul's attention to that gleaming plump flesh.

"Yessss," Saul hissed softly, resting a hand on Mateo's neck. "Kiss me."

As if that was a demand, Mateo went up on his toes, resting his hands on Saul's chest for balance.

It was all the invitation Saul needed, and his control shattered.

Swooping down, Saul captured Mateo's mouth. He pushed his tongue between his mate's slightly parted lips, accepting the invitation. In seconds, the flavor of the other half of his soul exploded across his taste buds, sending his senses soaring.

Wrapping his free hand around Mateo's hips, Saul palmed the man's firm ass cheek. He used his shifter strength to easily heft his human up, pressing his back against the SUV's side. Feeling Mateo wrap his legs around his waist and his arms around his neck, Saul growled into the other man's mouth.

Saul felt Mateo's answering hardness pressing against his own, and he became lost in the exquisite knowledge that he held his willing, eager mate in his arms.

That pleasure shattered when someone yelled, "Get a room, guys!"

CHAPTER THREE

Embarrassment flooded Mateo — for so many reasons. When Saul had kissed him, most of his thoughts had fled. Then Mateo had felt Saul's hand on his butt, and he was lifting him, pressing him into the SUV, and his arousal had swamped his brain.

Mateo had also been impressed with Saul's strength. He'd never had anyone lift him before.

I can't believe I climbed him like a tree. He must think I'm so easy.

When Saul lifted his head, breaking the kiss to look in the direction of the guy who'd hollered, Mateo tucked his face against Saul's shoulder. He peeked in the same direction. Out of the corner of his eye, Mateo spotted Saul's face as he glared at their interrupter.

Truthfully, it had probably been a good thing.

In response to Saul's angry look, the man just laughed and continued walking.

"A-At least he didn't, uh, heckle us," Mateo muttered.

Saul sighed before peering down at him, his features easing into a rueful expression. "He did interrupt the best damn kiss of my life though," he told him, his pale blue eyes pinning him with heat. "But he was right. This isn't the place for this." Then Saul grimaced as he shook his head. "Gods, I'm truly fucking this up. I shouldn't have mauled you."

As Saul spoke, he eased Mateo back to the ground.

And wow, that he was still holding me was really impressive.

Then Saul's words registered.

19

He thought kissing me was a mistake?

"My apologies," Saul continued with a shake of his head. His smile appeared tight as he held Mateo's gaze. "Will you forgive me?"

Cocking his head, Mateo asked, "You thought the best kiss of your life was a mistake?"

"No," Saul assured, sliding his hand up to cradle Mateo's nape. "I thought mauling you in public was a mistake." Wincing, he added, "And not very gentlemanly of me." Saul's thin lips pulled into a serious line. "Even though my actions don't portray it, I do want you as more than just a quick fuck." Grimacing, he shook his head. "Gods, I shouldn't use such coarse words with my mate. You're meant to be wooed."

Furrowing his brows, Mateo tried to follow Saul's rambling. "Y-You want me for more than, uh, just a night?"

Who uses the word woo anymore?

This guy, evidently.

Saul nodded once, quick and firm. "Yes." Teasing his fingers through Mateo's hair, he eased the strands away from his forehead. "I definitely want more with you."

"Why?" Mateo really wasn't following. "You don't even know me."

"Just like you don't know me," Saul countered. "But we'll change that," he stated firmly. Dipping his head, Saul pressed a quick kiss to the corner of Mateo's mouth. "Now then, let's get back to the plan. I'll take you home to freshen up and change." Saul reached to the right and opened the front passenger door. "Then I'll take you to dinner."

"Okay," Mateo agreed, following Saul's urging and getting into the seat.

To Mateo's surprise, Saul even reached in and did up his seatbelt.

That's . . . odd.

Mateo watched in silence as Saul closed the door then rounded the hood of the SUV. The tall man slipped behind the wheel and fired up the engine. As Saul started them on their way, obeying when Mateo told him to turn left, he took a second to glance around the vehicle.

Silently whistling under his breath, Mateo took a second to appreciate the SUV. The interior was nicely appointed, and he recognized the logo as a *BMW*. Mateo couldn't even guess how much a vehicle like this one would cost.

Expensive suit. Expensive SUV.

"Uh, so what do you do, Saul?" Mateo asked, trying to sound casual. "Oh, you'll need to turn left ahead." He pointed off to the side. "That's my apartment complex. Easy walking distance."

"I'm a lawyer," Saul answered, following Mateo's instruction. "I work exclusively for Kaiser Roush. Have you heard of him?"

Mateo gaped. "Yeah. Who hasn't heard of him?" With an embarrassed flush working up his neck, he admitted, "My father railed about the decline of good people when Mister Roush came out as living with a guy."

Saul grimaced, offering him a commiserating smile. "They don't approve of homosexuality, huh?" As Mateo shook his head, Saul parked in a visitor parking spot before turning to look at him. "Do they know you're gay, Mateo?"

With a deep sigh, Mateo nodded once. "Yeah. It, uh . . . didn't go well," he finished on a mumble.

"I'm sorry, sweetheart," Saul rumbled, reaching over to take his hand. "You'll find acceptance with Alpha Kaiser and our people."

Cocking his head even as he enjoyed the heat of Saul's hand in his own, Mateo asked, "Alpha Kaiser?" *That's an odd title.* "Why do you call him that?"

Saul opened his mouth, then snapped it shut again. To Mateo's surprise, he spotted the faintest hue of pink coloring Saul's neck, just above his tie. The man cleared his throat and peered away from him for a few seconds.

When Saul focused on him again, he offered him a tight smile. "You do make me forget myself," he stated enigmatically. "When we get to know each other better, then I'll explain." Saul squeezed Mateo's fingers and told him, "Please understand, I will explain, but that's for another time."

Mateo shrugged. "Okay." Realizing a subject change was needed, he asked, "So, you work with Kaiser Roush's team of lawyers?"

Saul smirked, pride filling his crystal blue eyes. "Actually, I'm Kaiser's *only* lawyer."

Gaping, Mateo couldn't help the way his eyes widened. A man of Kaiser Roush's stature normally had teams of lawyers. For Saul to be the only one, he had to be damn good.

Considering that, and taking in Saul's put-together figure, Mateo realized the man had to have a certain image to uphold.

Oh, God. He's so far out of my league.

As much as it hurt, Mateo had to admit the truth. "I can't go to dinner with you." Shaking his head, Mateo murmured, "I'm not good enough for you to be seen with. I'm a nobody."

Oh hell no.

Frowning at Mateo, Saul shook his head. "I don't know where you're getting that sort of idea, but get it out of your pretty little head right now," he ordered. Seeing the way Mateo's jaw sagged open, Saul did his best to soften his tone as he asked, "Why would you say such a thing?"

Saul needed his mate to open up to him, to share his concerns, and he could indeed scent Mateo's worry and concern. The scents were tamping down on his mate's arousal, and Saul didn't like it. He much preferred the rich earthiness of Mateo's need.

Needs I very much want to fulfill.

"Well, it's obvious," Mateo began softly, picking at his

jeans with his free hand. "I mean." He glanced away before giving Saul a side-eyed look. "You're a high-powered, high-profile lawyer. You can't be seen with someone like me. A lowly dishwasher."

"How you earn your money to pay your rent is no one's business but yours," Saul countered, doing his best to sound soothing. "You pay your bills, not expecting anything from anyone, and that's a lot more than some people."

Mateo still didn't look convinced. "Well, even you asked if I had any passions," he muttered, glancing away furtively for a few seconds. "Weren't you thinking the same thing? That I had to be aspiring to something other than washing dishes all my life?"

Saul winced, realizing his words could have been misconstrued that way. "That wasn't what I meant," he told his mate, squeezing his hand once more. "I just wondered if you had any hobbies or interests. I was looking for common ground."

After a few seconds of nibbling his bottom lip, Mateo admitted, "I like walking on the beach and collecting seashells." He cleared his throat, then opened his mouth before closing it again. Saul waited, and his patience was rewarded when Mateo admitted, "I like to glue them into shapes and paint them. I sell them online for a little extra cash."

Well, damn. My mate has an artist's soul.

Saul really liked that.

It also gave him a starting point on something they could do together.

"I know a beach that I'm certain you've never been to," Saul offered, thinking of several of the secluded beaches on land owned by his shifter pod. "You'll be able to find a number of unique shells there. When's your next day off work?"

After a few seconds of hesitation, Mateo answered, "Tuesday."

Saul bit back a grimace even as he nodded. It was Friday evening. He really didn't want to wait four days until he could see his mate again.

"Hmmm. What's your work's policy on boyfriends visiting employees during break?" Saul asked, arching one brow. "And what are your hours? I'd like to see you sooner than that."

"Boyfriend?" To Saul's relief, Mateo snickered. "Uh, we haven't even been on our first date, yet." His expression turned shy. "What if I chew with my mouth open or fart in public or do something else equally embarrassing to you?"

Saul smirked. "Do you do those things?" he asked, amusement filling him.

"Well, no." Mateo quickly added, "Not on purpose anyway. I mean, everyone does something like that on occasion by accident."

"Indeed, they do," Saul agreed. Using a cajoling tone, he added, "Now then, how about you head up to your apartment, and I'll return in" — he glanced at the clock on the dash of his SUV — "just over an hour. Then we'll go on our first date, and I'll officially become your boyfriend." Ignoring Mateo's disbelieving expression, Saul pressed, "That work for you, cutie?"

"Um, o-okay."

While Saul could scent — and tell by Mateo's expression — that his mate still didn't understand what Saul could see in him, he would explain . . . in time. He leaned over the center console while moving his free hand to cradle Mateo's nape. Saul settled his lips over his human's and took a short taste, enjoying his unique flavor.

Before Saul could get carried away, he broke the kiss. "See you soon, Mateo," he stated huskily as he released his mate.

"See you soon," Mateo repeated, the human's voice sounding breathless. Then he slipped from the vehicle.

Saul watched, smiling, pleased to see Mateo look over his shoulder at him while crossing the parking lot. The fact that a driver had to slam on his brakes because Mateo wasn't watching where he was going wasn't such a good thing. Still, Saul was pleased he distracted his mate so much.

Next time, I'll walk him to the door.

Hmm . . . which apartment is his? I don't even have his phone number to check.

Shaking his head at his foolish oversight, Saul pulled out his phone and called Ovram. The sea lion shifter was their pod's hacking guru. Saul felt certain Ovram would be able to help him.

"Hey, Saul," Ovram greeted. "You almost here? We're set up in the green conference room. Alpha wants to hear what Detective Grisham had to say, but the detective got hung up at work. Can we hear it from you?"

Saul winced, mentally smacking himself upside the head. He couldn't believe that he'd forgotten about the meeting he'd had with the detective that morning. Finding his mate had completely pushed any other thought out of Saul's mind.

"Uh, no, actually," Saul admitted. "I'm not even close to home." After a second of hesitation, he added, "And I won't be back for, well, I'm not certain when I'll be back."

"Putting you on speaker," Ovram told him. A second later, Saul could hear the sounds of others in the room. "Go ahead, Alpha."

"You completely forgot about this meeting, didn't you?" Alpha Kaiser asked, amusement lacing his tone. "Does this have to do with finding your mate?"

Relieved that their alpha was such an understanding guy, Saul admitted, "I did, and it is." With a chuckle, he stated, "I should have known Beta William would pass my news onto you." Saul had called the beta—who happened to be Alpha Kaiser's younger brother—when he'd needed advice on wooing his mate. "Mateo just got off his shift twenty minutes ago, and I drove him home. We're going to dinner in an hour."

"You with him right now?" Alpha Kaiser asked.

At the same time, Ovram hollered, "Hot damn. Congrats, Saul. That's awesome!"

"Thanks, Ovram." Saul grinned as he relaxed in his seat. "I feel truly blessed that the Fates have finally seen fit to gift me with my mate." Answering his alpha's question, Saul told him, "No. I'm sitting in my SUV in the parking lot of his apartment complex. I actually called Ovram because I need to know his apartment number." With a deprecating snort, Saul admitted, "I forgot to ask him."

Alpha Kaiser's deep chuckle sounded through the line. "Finding your mate can do that to a man," he commented.

Ovram snickered. "Yep." Saul could hear the tapping of keys as he asked, "Okay. Mateo what?"

Saul opened his mouth, then snapped it closed again. He frowned. "Uh, I don't know." He could feel his cheeks beginning to heat, and he was ever-so-grateful to be alone.

Gods. I don't remember the last time I blushed.

Laughing again, Ovram fired off a few questions. "Okay. What *do* you know? What apartment complex are you at? Where does he work?"

Reclining his seat, Saul answered the sea lion shifter's questions. It only took the man a minute to pull up information on his mate—Mateo Barrera. He learned his mate's apartment number, how long he'd worked at the coffee shop, as well as his age—twenty-four.

Saul also learned that just three months before, his parents had blocked his phone number, as had most of the rest of the family. While he figured that had to have hurt his kind-hearted human, he knew it was better for him. It meant he wouldn't have to deal with meddling family.

Plus, I can give him a new family. One that'll accept him for who he is.

With that thought in mind, Saul spent the rest of the phone call discussing the fact that Armando Whitney—a man who'd not only tried to have Alpha Kaiser, but Beta William, killed—

more than once—had somehow managed to make bail—and he was now missing.

How does some of the key evidence go conveniently missing?

Right. Easy answer. Corruption.

CHAPTER FOUR

True to Saul's word, Mateo heard his doorbell ring at exactly five-thirty.

Mateo hesitated for a few seconds, wiping his sweaty palms on his clean jeans. After taking a quick breath and giving himself a mental pep-talk, he headed to the door and opened it. His breath caught in his throat as he took in Saul's sexy frame.

Geez, what does this man see in me?

Saul had removed his suit jacket along with his tie. He'd unbuttoned the top couple of buttons on his long-sleeve shirt, revealing his slender throat. The view caused Mateo's mouth to water with his desire to suck on Saul's prominent Adam's apple.

Damn, I'd love to mark him.

"I'd let you," Saul rumbled, his ice-blue eyes narrowing.

Mateo gasped. "D-Did I say that out loud?"

A sensual smile curved Saul's thin lips. "Yes, Mateo. Yes, you did." Stalking through the doorway toward him, Saul told him, "And to be fair, I have every intention of marking you, too."

Then Saul slipped his arms around Mateo's waist and pulled him close.

Mateo was only too happy to be there, and he rested his palms on Saul's chest. While the taller man had a slender frame, there was still plenty of defined muscle beneath Mateo's fingers. He wondered if Saul had to work out to stay in such great shape, considering he had what most considered a desk job.

"Can't resist when you look at me like that," Saul rumbled before bending and sealing his mouth over Mateo's.

Feeling Saul's tongue touch his bottom lip, Mateo opened happily. He welcomed the taller man's appendage. Flicking out his own, Mateo ran it along Saul's and moaned into the other man's mouth as he enjoyed his deep masculine flavor.

Long before Mateo wanted Saul to, the other man ended the kiss and lifted his head. Mateo didn't care what his air-deprived lungs were telling him. It didn't even matter that he was a little light-headed.

Mateo would have been willing to let Saul ravish his mouth all night.

Mmmm . . . a night with Saul. What would that be like?

While Mateo wasn't a virgin, he wouldn't consider himself the most experienced guy, either. Somehow, he knew that getting into bed with Saul would be like nothing he'd ever before experienced. Mateo could hardly wait, and his erection ached with anticipation behind his fly.

Saul drew in a deep breath before letting out a low growl. His pale blue eyes appeared to almost glow with a light of their own. He stared at him with a feral smile as his nostrils flared.

"Damn, Mateo," Saul rumbled. "It's so damn hard to be a gentleman with you."

Upon seeing Saul's hungry expression and feeling the squeeze of his fingers on his hips, Mateo felt a surge of boldness. "Maybe." He hesitated an instant, peering up at Saul through his lashes. Girding up his courage, he stated, "Maybe I don't want a gentleman."

Letting out another groan, Saul squeezed his hips once, twice. Then he bent and pressed a hard, closed-mouth kiss to Mateo's lips. When he straightened, he eased his grip and took a step backward.

"But you deserve a gentleman," Saul told him. After another deep breath, betrayed by the way his lean torso expanded and contracted, Saul released his sides only to take Mateo's hand in his own. "Ready? Do you need to get anything?" Saul's gaze raked over Mateo's frame with a heated look. "You look magnificent, by the way. Love the way those jeans hug your gorgeous bubble butt."

"Th-Thank you," Mateo stuttered, feeling the warmth of a blush threaten to darken his cheeks. He wasn't even certain when Saul would have had a chance to check out his butt in his jeans, but he didn't question the man. Instead, Mateo told him, "Uh, no. I have everything."

Mateo had grabbed his keys and wallet from his dresser when he'd heard the doorbell ring.

"Unless you think I'll need a jacket?" Mateo asked.

Saul shook his head, tugging him toward the still-open door. "No." As he shut the door behind them, he winked at Mateo. "But if I'm wrong and you get chilled, I'll keep you warm, my mate."

"Mate," Mateo repeated, allowing Saul to pull him toward the elevator. As they entered the carriage—it had opened as soon as Saul had hit the down button—he commented, "You called me that before."

"I did, and I will again. Probably often," Saul told him, wrapping his arm possessively around his shoulders while hitting the button for the ground floor. "For now, consider it a pet name. An endearment. I'll explain its deeper meaning when we know each other better."

Mateo nodded as they exited the elevator. While he was tempted to press for more information, he realized they hardly knew each other. A few kisses did not a relationship make.

Keeping that in mind, Mateo changed the subject. "So, uh, where are we going?" He glanced down at his clothes—his jeans and a nice polo shirt—before checking out Saul's suit pants and button-down top. "I should have asked before. Am I dressed okay?"

"You're dressed amazingly," Saul told him, opening the passenger door for him before placing a hand on Mateo's upper arm and helping him in. "And I looked a few places up on my phone. Here. Why don't you tell me what you prefer?"

Saul handed Mateo his phone before closing the door and walking around the hood.

Mateo scrolled over the map of the area. Saul had flagged three different restaurants, all within a twenty-minute drive. He smiled at the selections, familiar with two while realizing the third might be a little high-class for a first date. Although the thought was nice.

After Saul settled behind the wheel and started the SUV, he turned his attention to Mateo. "Preference?"

Handing back the phone, Mateo asked, "Would it be totally cliché to ask to go to the Mexican place?" He hurried to explain, "I know that one makes amazing empanadas, and I absolutely love them."

Saul nodded. "Sure. Never been there and love to try new foods," he told him as he transferred the address to his SUV's navigation.

As they traveled, their conversation turned to light things. Saul asked about Mateo's shell collecting. When Mateo admitted he loved whale watching, Saul offered to take him out on his boat.

"I know a few absolutely magnificent locations," Saul told him with a grin. "You'll love them."

Mateo found himself agreeing without a second thought. It was only a few seconds after that he realized that meant he'd just scheduled a second date with the handsome man. He barely managed to keep from grinning like an idiot.

Upon reaching the restaurant, Saul once again rested his

hand proprietarily on Mateo's lower back as he guided him toward the place. He opened the door for him, allowing him to enter first. When the host offering seating asked if they wanted a booth or a table, Saul peered beyond the man, openly surveying the room.

"I'd like that table, please," Saul told the man with a small smile. "If it's available."

The man glanced over his shoulder to see where Saul indicated before refocusing on him. "Of course, sir." Then he led the way toward where Saul wanted.

Mateo felt a flutter in his gut when he saw that it was one of the square, four-person tables set near the back. It offered a bit of privacy but didn't make Mateo feel like he was being hidden away. Saul reinforced that feeling when he pulled a chair back for Mateo before taking the seat directly to his left, placing Saul's own back against the far wall.

Just as Mateo settled in his chair, he felt his bladder twinge. As soon as the host left, telling them their server would be with them soon, he told Saul, "I'm going to slip to the men's room." As Mateo rose, he murmured, "Be right back."

Saul smiled up at him and grabbed his hand in a loose hold. "Would you like to share a bottle of wine with me?"

"Uh, sure." Mateo had never had wine at the restaurant before, but he thought that sounded like a very date-like thing. Still, he had to warn, "I'm not much of a wine connoisseur, so I'll try whatever you decide."

"Fair enough." Saul squeezed his palm once more before telling him with a wink, "If you don't end up liking it, there's always margaritas."

Mateo chuckled. Smiling, he squeezed Saul's hand back, liking that the man didn't seem to mind light public displays of affection. Then he pulled free and hustled to the nearby men's room.

After using the urinal, Mateo moved to the sink. He was

washing his hands when he heard the door behind him open and close, the hinges squeaking softly. Grabbing a paper towel and drying his hands, Mateo turned to furtively peer at who'd entered . . . and froze.

"Emilio," Mateo whispered, recognizing his fourteen-year-old nephew.

"Hi, Uncle Mateo."

Hearing Emilio's whispered words, seeing his nephew's pensive expression, Mateo acted on instinct and opened his arms to welcome the gangly teenager into a hug. For an instant, Emilio just continued to stare at him. Mateo was about to put his arms down when his nephew dove into his embrace, wrapping his skinny arms around his body in a tight hug.

Mateo returned the boy's hug, his heart racing a mile a minute. He'd always had a special bond with Emilio. The boy was his eldest brother's oldest son. His brother — Santiago — had married his wife at twenty, and Emilio had arrived a year later. Mateo and Emilio were only ten years apart, and he'd been the best uncle he could be.

"I miss you," Emilio whispered against his chest.

"I miss you, too," Mateo replied, rubbing his hand up and down Emilio's back. Still, he had to wonder, "Are you here with family?"

Emilio nodded, his cheek rubbing against Mateo's polo shirt. "Dad and the others didn't notice you when you came in, but I did." Easing back, he peered up at Mateo, his lower lip caught between his teeth. His brows were furrowed in a pensive expression as he asked, "Is that guy you're with, uh, is he your b-boyfriend?"

"Well, it may be a little early to call him that," Mateo replied, knowing he needed to be honest with his nephew. "But I'm hoping it's headed that way."

Frowning a little, Emilio mumbled, "So, you're really

gay?"

"Yeah, Emilio," Mateo confirmed, wondering if that would make Emilio run, but he refused to hide any longer. "I didn't lie. I'm gay."

Emilio blew out a deep breath. Peering up at Mateo, he swallowed hard, then blurted, "I'm gay, too."

Well shit.

Recalling Mateo's comment about enjoying the restaurant's empanadas, when Saul spotted the mini-empanada appetizer dish, he ordered it along with a bottle of Riesling. He knew the light wine would pair well if Mateo ended up getting something spicy. It helped that it was a brand Saul was familiar with and knew he enjoyed.

Saul spotted movement to his left and watched Mateo exit the hallway to the men's room. A young man was with him, Although Saul wasn't the best at guessing ages, he surmised the male couldn't be too far into puberty. He also had the same dark hair and eyes as Mateo, as well as skin tone.

Hmmm . . . family?

The young man glanced toward the other side of the restaurant before giving Mateo a quick hug. Then he hurried off. Mateo watched him for a second, his expression troubled, before returning to their table.

"Something wrong?" Saul asked, having no qualms about being nosy when it came to his mate. After all, he could smell a hint of spice in Mateo's scent that bespoke of the man's agitation.

Mateo eased into his seat and offered a tight smile. "Um, sorry. That was my nephew. Emilio." His brows remained drawn as he rested his forearms on the table and met Saul's gaze. His voice was low when he murmured, "Emilio just told me he's gay." Shaking his head, Mateo continued, "If my brother finds out . . ." His words trailed off, and a fresh wave of unease filled Saul's nostrils.

"Will they kick him out?" Saul asked, reaching over and placing his hand over Mateo's wrist. He rested his thumb on his mate's pulse point, rubbing lightly. "How old is he?"

Sighing deeply, Mateo seemed to start relaxing under that small contact. "He's only fourteen. I'd hate to think my brother would be so callous as to kick Emilio out, but I have to admit it's a possibility." He met Saul's gaze, his expression appearing pained. "My family's very religious. What if my family decided to send him to one of those conversion therapy camps?" Mateo's eyes gleamed, telling of his worry just as much as his scent. "I couldn't stand to think of Emilio in a horrible place like that. He's a sweet kid."

"We won't let anything like that happen to him," Saul declared calmly. Upon seeing Mateo's brows shoot up and scenting his surprise, Saul offered him a wry grin. "I *am* a lawyer, you know. And while child custody rights are not my area of expertise, I have many contacts." Thinking of the sort of place Mateo mentioned—a supposed camp that essentially brainwashed or tortured teenagers who didn't meet the accepted standards of their family's beliefs or religion—he declared with a growl in his voice, "I'm of the belief that sending your child to a place like that is abuse. We won't let that happen to him."

One way or another.

If Mateo's family threatened that kind of behavior, Saul knew his mate would need plenty of support. Fortunately, his pod would offer it in a heartbeat. Saul would need to talk to his alpha about the best tactics.

For a few seconds, Mateo appeared hopeful. Then his face fell as he shook his head. "I just met you," he stated. "I can't drag you into my family drama." Before Saul could counter Mateo, his mate quickly added, "Besides, I could just be overreacting. They disowned me only a few short months ago, so the wounds are still fresh." Forcing a smile, Mateo met his gaze. "Anyway, I reminded Emilio that my phone number hasn't changed, and if he needs to talk to me, he can call anytime." With a shrug, he continued, "Emilio says he doesn't intend to come out anytime soon or anything. He just really needed someone to talk to about it." Blatantly changing the subject, Mateo asked, "So, what wine did you decide on?"

Saul nodded slowly, allowing the change. "A Riesling that I enjoy. It pairs well with spicy food." While Mateo nodded, his attention falling to the menu, Saul would guess that his mate didn't actually care. Saul squeezed his wrist lightly. "I also ordered the empanada appetizer. You said they were good here."

That brought Mateo's attention back to Saul. His dark eyes brightened, filling with appreciation. He began smiling again, anticipation in his expression.

"Yum. Thanks!"

Deciding that was a much better look on Mateo's features, Saul vowed to do what he could to put it there often.

"Absolutely," Saul replied with a smile of his own. Returning his attention to his own menu, he asked, "So, what else is good here?"

As Saul listened to Mateo discuss menu options, he thought about the text he was going to send Ovram. He intended to ask their tech guru to do a deep dive into Mateo's family.

Just in case.

CHAPTER FIVE

Dinner tasted amazing, and Mateo found himself enjoying Saul's dry humor. The man shared stories of his friends' antics, as well as how they met their current partners. The tales drew Mateo out of the funk running into Emilio had pulled him into.

Even the glare Mateo saw Santiago send his way when his brother was leaving didn't lower his spirits.

While part of Mateo thought spending time with someone new shouldn't have been so easy, he couldn't deny that it was. The conversation between them flowed smoothly, one story running into the next. Saul told about a few funny case highlights, while Mateo admitted to his utter inability to run the coffee café's machines. Even admitting his epic fail at making a frappe, causing the foam to spray all over the place — including himself and a fellow co-worker — had been the icing on the cake.

"So, yeah. I don't mind being the dishwasher," Mateo admitted, feeling a little heat in his cheeks. "So much easier than trying to figure that stuff out."

Saul chuckled, the sound deep and low. "I bet you were a sight after that." With a smirk, he waggled his thin eyebrows. "At least you'll never have to worry about trying to impress me with your coffee making abilities."

Mateo barked a laugh, grinning. "Right. Since you don't like coffee."

"Exactly." Saul picked up the nearly empty bottle of wine. "Want the last of it?"

After a second of hesitation, Mateo did his best to act coy. "Are you trying to get me tipsy so you can take advantage of me?"

Saul's blue eyes filled with heat as he slowly lowered the bottle to the table. Leaning forward, he rumbled huskily, "Oh, my dear Mateo." His thin lips curved into a smile that caused the hairs on Mateo's neck to stand on end. "There will be no taking advantage of you. I promise you that I want you fully cognizant when the time comes." Saul chuckled, the sound husky and low. "And it will come . . . soon, if what you said earlier about not wanting me to be a gentleman was true."

Mateo felt as if his heart skipped a beat in his chest. His throat suddenly went dry. He grabbed his wine glass and took a large sip, finishing what was in there.

"Yes," Mateo forced out, his voice coming out husky. He felt warmth churn in his gut, and he knew it wasn't the wine. Mateo hadn't had that much. Instead, the heat was all arousal, and his jeans felt uncomfortably tight. "I was telling the truth."

Humming, Saul poured the wine into Mateo's glass. It didn't even fill it a quarter. "I'll track down the server," he told him, rising to his feet. Giving Mateo a sultry look before walking away, Saul stated, "Then we'll see what un-gentlemanly pursuits we can get up to this evening."

Mateo nodded as he watched Saul stop at a different server. His date said something to him while holding up a card before moving to the front where a cash register rested. He was obviously waiting for the server to track down their bill.

His heart racing in his chest, Mateo focused on his breathing. He enjoyed the rest of the wine as well as a few more chips and salsa. Saul had enjoyed the warm chips and spicy salsa so much that they'd ended up getting two refills. It had amazed Mateo to see Saul pack so much away. The tall, slender man seemed to have a hollow leg.

After finishing the wine, Mateo rose and headed toward the front. Saul was just finishing scribbling his signature on the receipt, and he looked up and gave him an appreciative once-over. His ice-blue eyes gleamed in the restaurant lighting, telling Mateo that Saul must have enjoyed what he saw.

The look once again caused Mateo's blood to burn. There was no denying what Saul intended to happen when they reached Mateo's apartment. His intentions were written clearly in that look alone before he cleared it and held out a hand to Mateo.

Am I really doing this?

Yes. Yes, I am.

Even if all Saul's sweet words about a relationship were bogus, Mateo wanted what the man was offering.

Even if it's for just one night.

Saul made Mateo feel alive, wanted and desired, in a way that he'd never before experienced. After taking him the iced chai tea and meeting the sort of man Saul obviously usually went for, he'd worried that he would never get a chance at the man. Mateo still didn't truly believe all of Saul's flowery words, but he was willing to risk it.

Everything in life is a risk.

Once again, Saul opened the door for him and guided him into the seat. He quickly rounded the vehicle, appearing to be typing on his phone as he went. Saul climbed in and dropped the device into a cupholder before buckling up and starting them on their way.

"On Tuesday, I'll take you out on a boat," Saul told him, reaching over and taking Mateo's hand. He even went so far as to thread their fingers together. "Do you enjoy water skiing, scuba diving, or snorkeling?"

"Um, I've never been able to get up on skis," Mateo admitted. "But when I was a kid, my parents rented a boat on a lake, and they pulled us kids behind it on a big inflated banana."

Saul chuckled, nodding. "I've seen those. Never tried it myself." Casting a grin Mateo's way, he offhandedly said, "I just may have to pick one up."

Mateo gaped a little as he stared at Saul, surprise flooding him. The man said it so casually, as if spending a few hundred bucks on a banana raft was no big deal. A trickle of unease hit him as Mateo realized . . . for Saul, it probably wasn't.

As Saul pulled into the parking lot of Mateo's apartment complex, Mateo knew he was in way over his head with Saul. Except, heading up to his apartment, he didn't know what to do about it . . . if anything. Mateo had longed for the man from afar for weeks.

And now he's here . . . with me. I'll worry about the fact that I'll probably get my heart broken later.

Then Mateo was opening the front door, heading inside, and a second later, Saul was on him. As he was lifted into the shockingly strong man's arms, his mouth captured, and kissed to within an inch of his life, all worries and concerns fled Mateo's mind.

Saul knew that Mateo was starting to overthink things. He needed his mate to relax, to forget all his concerns and worries. To that end, Saul did what he knew would work.

The second Mateo was in the apartment and Saul had the door closed and locked behind him, he swept his human into his arms and kissed him. Just like the last time Saul'd had Mateo in his arms, his human sank into his embrace. While Saul knew that Mateo didn't understand the magnetism between them, his mate didn't fight it.

Just as it should be.

Sliding one arm around Mateo's back, Saul slipped the other under his ass. He palmed the full mound while tightening his arms and lifting. With an easy flex of his shifter muscles, Saul brought Mateo off his feet and against his body.

To Saul's distinct pleasure—after feeding him a squeak of surprise—Mateo wrapped his legs around Saul's waist. He clutched his mate close and began prowling through the apartment, searching for Mateo's bedroom. All the while, he feasted on the sweet essence that was Mateo's mouth.

Saul figured it couldn't be a big space, but he still managed to bump into a sofa arm and a wall. Breaking the kiss, he let out a laugh, surprising himself. He couldn't remember the last time he'd felt such mirth with a lover. Upon seeing Mateo's panting flushed face and kiss-swollen lips, Saul grinned with satisfaction.

"You're gorgeous, Mateo," Saul rumbled, reveling in the fact that he'd put that look on his mate's face. His human's dark eyes shown with lust, and his pupils were blown. His naturally bronze cheeks were flushed darker. Seeing Mateo shake his head, as if in denial, Saul growled, "Yes, you are. Fucking gorgeous." Saul took that moment to glance around, spotting three doors. "Where's your bedroom?"

"L-Left one," Mateo told him on a panting breath.

Without waiting for an invitation, Saul stalked over to it. He twisted the hand he had on Mateo's back while bending a little at the knees so he could open the door. Stalking inside, he didn't bother with the lights.

Saul's keen shifter eyesight allowed him to make out damn near everything perfectly fine. Plus, the glow from the streetlights outside would offer the same to Mateo. Instead, Saul focused on the queen-sized bed and headed toward it.

Placing Mateo in the middle of the bed with his head on a pillow, Saul quickly reached for his feet. "You fire my blood in a way I've never thought possible," he muttered, tugging off his human's shoes and socks. "Never felt like this before." Saul figured Mateo didn't believe him. A human wouldn't understand the mate-pull . . . the driving need between them. "Lift your arms," Saul ordered, reaching for the hem of his polo shirt. He would explain everything to his mate . . . in time.

Seeing Mateo's hesitation, Saul took a breath. His cock throbbed behind the fly of his slacks, and he knew he tented them obscenely. Saul didn't traditionally wear underwear, so there was nothing but the thin material to contain his aching erection, and it would show.

"Lift your arms, Mateo," Saul urged again, sliding the palm of his left hand under the fabric. He caressed his soon-to-be lover's belly, relishing the soft flesh there. "Let me see you."

Mateo slowly lifted his arms.

Saul took complete advantage. Carefully, he tugged up his human's shirt. He eased it over his head and off his arms. With his attention riveted on the stunning human on the rumpled, dark-green sheets, Saul felt his breath catch.

In a word, Saul thought Mateo was absolutely stunning.

And I don't even have him naked yet.

When Mateo crossed his arms over his chest and looked away, shyness in the move, Saul yanked his head out of his ass.

Gotta reassure my love.

"No, baby," Saul crooned, easing his palms under Mateo's arms. He gently urged him to relax his arms. "I find you stunning, my mate." Saul couldn't have stopped the possessive words if he'd tried. "You're everything I could ever want and more."

While speaking, Saul gripped one of Mateo's wrists and lifted it. He brought his human's palm to his lips and pressed a kiss to the center. With his other hand, he reached for his own fly.

"I've waited so long to meet someone like you, Mateo," Saul told his human.

Not someone like you, but you.

Saul couldn't tell Mateo that, yet, though. Instead, he worked his own belt and fly open swiftly. Instantly, his long slender shaft burst free between the flaps. He heard Mateo's sharply indrawn breath while watching his mate's eyes widen. Saul knew what Mateo saw. His erection matched his body type. He wasn't thick by any means, but he was long — a smidge over eleven inches, to be exact.

"Don't worry, Mateo," Saul crooned, drawing Mateo's attention even as he shoved his slacks down his legs. He quickly shucked his shoes and socks with them, leaving himself just in his long-sleeved dress shirt. *Huh. Been a while since I've been so eager that I undressed out of order.* Smiling at Mateo, Saul dismissed the oddity from his mind. Instead, he began working his cufflinks while grinning at Mateo. "Where's your lube, my mate?" When he saw his human hesitate, he added, "And remember, we don't have to do anything you don't want." As Saul set the cufflinks on the nightstand, he skimmed the fingertips of his other hand up his mate's inner thigh, scraping over the denim cloth. "I'll even just take the opportunity to only hold you, if that's your wish."

Even if my dick would hate me.

For my mate, I'll deal with it.

Mateo cleared his voice before peering at him through his lashes. Something that Saul was coming to realize was a tell of true shyness.

My sweet human.

"I-I want this," Mateo told him. "Want you." He nibbled his bottom lip for just a second before reaching for the fly of his jeans. "J-Just, um, been a while. Go slow?" As Mateo stared at Saul's length, he muttered, "N-Never taken anything so, uh, long."

Saul offered Mateo a predator's smile. "Yes, Mateo. I'll take such good care of you."

Besides, Saul knew that Mateo would be able to take him. The human was his mate, after all. If the man needed a little extra patience, Saul could certainly give him that.

Anything for my mate.

Mateo nodded, seeming to accept. "Nightstand." He pointed to the drawer of the cabinet where Saul had just left his cufflinks. Then he began wiggling his hips and shimmying out of his jeans.

Saul barely managed to keep from swallowing his tongue as the rest of Mateo's thick-set body was revealed to him. His legs were strong with clearly defined muscles. Sure, he sported a bit of extra padding around the middle, but that didn't detract from his stunning physique.

Instead, Saul appreciated that he would have more to hold onto. Plus, it helped ease his fear that he might hurt his human mate. No, in Saul's mind, the muscles on his body and extra weight made Mateo absolutely perfect.

Plus, the thick, seven-inch erection jutting from Mateo's groin made Saul's mouth water, just begging to be sucked.

Hell, yeah.

Saul yanked his attention away from Mateo's stunning body and tugged open the drawer. If it weren't for the built-in safety stop, he would have sent it crashing to the floor in his eagerness. Fighting back a blush—something he hadn't done in more years than he could count—Saul searched for the lube.

Right on top.

Grinning, Saul grabbed the item, slammed the drawer back shut, and climbed onto the bed with his mate. Eager in a way that Saul couldn't ever remember being, he reached for Mateo.

At last.

CHAPTER SIX

Seeing Saul's appreciative raking gaze, easily made out with the glow caused by the city lights through the window, helped banish Mateo's nerves. The man's expression told him that Saul truly liked what he was seeing. On top of that, the way the tall man's long, slender cock bobbed and leaked at his groin couldn't be faked.

Saul wants me.

"Gods, you're so fucking sexy, Mateo," Saul muttered, levering over him. "And all mine."

Saul pressed a hard kiss to Mateo's lips, stalling his natural reaction to counter his new lover's words. A second later, Saul began raining sucking kisses and nips down his jaw, along his neck, and across his shoulder. His hands were busy caressing the flesh of Mateo's arms, chest, stomach, and hips.

Everywhere Saul touched, Mateo felt as if his nerve endings came alive. The hairs on his arms stood on end. His nipples beaded. Goose bumps erupted over his flesh. Even his belly trembled when Saul raked calloused palms over it.

Oh gods! A lawyer with callouses. How?

The thought flitted in and out of Mateo's mind so fast, he had no chance of voicing it. Especially when Saul's mouth reached his groin. In one swift move, Saul swallowed Mateo's dick to the root.

Barking Saul's name, Mateo arched, his body bowing. Unable to help himself, he pressed his heels into the mattress and shoved up into Saul's face. Saul sucked hard even as he gripped Mateo's hips, easing him back onto the mattress.

45

Mateo whimpered and shuddered, his dick spurting a bead of pre-cum at the stronger man's move. His new lover continued to suck, bobbing slowly and sensually on his erection, causing blissful tingles to work down his shaft to his groin . . . and his balls. Mateo shifted his hips a little, but even when Saul moved one hand away, he still couldn't move much.

"Oh god," Mateo whined. Never had he felt such exquisite fellatio. His balls were quickly tightening, and he shuddered with a strange desire to push Saul away and to buck up deeper into the man's exquisite mouth. "Saul!"

Saul growled, adding another dimension to Mateo's pleasure-inducing dilemma. The vibrations swiftly swept down his length, settling in his balls. Mateo tried his best to untangle his tongue, but at that second, he felt Saul slide a slick finger deep into his channel, gliding over his prostate with unerring precision.

In the next instant, Mateo was coming. His orgasm roared through him, swamping his system and causing his senses to sing. A noise erupted from Mateo that he never recalled making before as he let out a sound between a whimper, screech, and bark.

Mateo heard the noise, hardly processing that it came from his own throat. Then he was floating in ecstasy. His brain felt as if it was fuzzing out and shivers racked his body. He trembled and shuddered, enjoying pulse after pulse of bliss-inducing pleasure.

"S-Saul," Mateo mumbled when his orgasm began to wind down. Except, he still felt on edge, as if his body was missing something. That was when Mateo realized Saul still had a finger—or maybe more—in his ass, working his channel and teasing at his prostate, keeping him on edge. Whining, Mateo twitched under Saul's ministrations, pleading, "P-Please."

A second later, Saul popped off Mateo's still-hard prick,

causing cool air to caress his overly sensitive length. "I got you, baby," Saul assured, rubbing a hand over his thigh, up his side, and along his stomach. "Gonna flip you, my mate," Saul rumbled. "Make it easier for you."

Mateo could barely focus as he blinked blearily at Saul.

"Ready?"

It took a few seconds for Mateo to realize that Saul was waiting for confirmation. The fact that the sexy, rich, high-powered lawyer who'd just sucked him off pulled his fingers free of his chute helped him focus just a little. Mateo still had to swallow a couple of times before he managed to answer.

"Y-Yes," Mateo murmured, gulping once more. "I-I w-want you." As Saul began levering up, his cock came on display, and Mateo couldn't help but stare. Saul's erection—so long and slender, but with a little bit of girth that he knew would make him feel it later—made Mateo's desire ramp up. "Oh, god, yes." With his brain feeling like mush from his epic orgasm, Mateo couldn't keep his thoughts to himself. "God, yes, I want to feel your long shaft drilling me so damn bad."

Saul let out a sound that was a mixture of groan and growl. "Fuck, baby," he snarled. "The things you say."

Leaning down, Saul pressed a hard, searching kiss to Mateo's lips. He thrust his tongue deep, allowing Mateo to taste himself on Saul's tongue. Then Saul jerked away, hissing in the process. Saul gripped Mateo's hips and used strength that still boggled Mateo's mind to flip him onto his stomach. A second later, Mateo felt Saul lever over him, the crown of his prick tapping at his entrance.

Mateo opened his mouth, knowing he should be asking about . . . something.

Except, a second later, Saul tucked his chin over Mateo's shoulder, nuzzling him. "Push out," his lover ordered. "Let me in, baby." An instant later, Saul followed that up with, "Let me give us both what we need."

"Yessss," Mateo hissed, wanting that, too. He struggled to get his shaking limbs to work, getting his knees and elbows under him. "Yes, please."

"Damn, my mate," Saul hissed, even as he began applying pressure to his most intimate of openings. He growled, placing one hand on Mateo's hip, his other holding up his weight. "Push out." Saul nipped his ear before purring once more, "Push out, Mateo."

Mateo did as he was told and pushed out. Within seconds, he felt Saul's swollen knob slip inside him. He gasped at the feel of hot flesh burrowing into his body, and his brain finally supplied a single word.

Condom.

Except, a second later, Mateo felt Saul's cock head slide across his prostate before moving deeper. The sparks flooded his groin, radiating out in waves of tingling pleasure, intensified by the way Saul eased his prick partway out before sliding deeper. Mateo whimpered and shivered, his senses blanketed by floating tingles that made him shudder and cry, not certain which way was up.

Mateo dug his fingers into the sheet beneath him, certain that if he let go, he would somehow float away. The heat of Saul's body along his backside kept him grounded. The man's steady thrust and retreat caused his senses to sing over each pass of his prostate.

Never had Mateo felt the like of it. He desperately wanted release as well as for the sensations to never end. Except, that wasn't possible, and he knew it, and his body finally erupted in a flash-fire of epic proportions.

For the second time that night, Mateo succumbed to the ecstasy of orgasm. He whimpered Saul's name, never recalling such a sensation as he floated with shivering tendrils of bliss. His breath came in short pants, and he did his best to get enough air into his lungs even as he floated on the heady wave of endorphins.

"S-Saul."

"Ready for one more, my mate?" Saul purred into his ear. "One more orgasm as I make you all mine."

Unable to imagine that, with his body still humming from his last release, Mateo could only accept. "A-Anything," he whispered.

Mateo's heart thudded wildly when he heard Saul's throat growl. That was followed by the feel of sharp teeth pricking the skin where his neck met his shoulder. He blinked in surprise, only to hiss with the pain of those same sharp teeth sinking into his flesh.

An instant later, the pain disappeared. It morphed into the most exquisite bliss Mateo had ever experienced. His nipples tingled as the zings of the bite traveled down his body. He sucked in a sharp breath when those sensations hit his groin.

He couldn't stop the cry of bliss as he once again succumbed to the pleasure of orgasm. His dick twitched and throbbed, sending pleasure through him. At the same time, he vaguely realized that he wasn't actually shooting, his balls having run dry.

Panting, soft and deep, Mateo struggled to catch his breath. Spots danced across his vision. His limbs trembled, barely keeping him up.

When Mateo felt Saul ease his teeth — actual teeth — out of his flesh, he whined at the odd sensation, his arms buckling.

"Easy, my mate," Saul purred into his ear, catching him, holding him tight against his chest. He stroked his hand down Mateo's body. "I'll take care of you. Just relax."

Mateo sighed as he allowed Saul to ease him sideways, away from what must have been a hell of a wet spot. A grunt escaped him when he felt his lover ease his prick from his body. As odd as that always felt to him, when he felt the cum trickling from him, that felt even odder.

It also finally reminded him of his earlier thought.

"We forgot a condom," Mateo whispered, uncertainty thrumming through him.

After all, Mateo had seen Saul's hook-up. The lawyer was a playboy.

Wasn't he?

"Relax, Mateo," Saul murmured, pressing a kiss to the back of his neck. "I'm clean. We're fine. I'd never put you at risk."

Mateo grunted in acknowledgement. He figured he would have questions later, but he couldn't seem to think of them. After all, his brain had been turned to mush by a triple orgasm.

"Go to sleep, my mate," Saul urged with another kiss. "I'll clean us up." After another peck, he urged, "Just rest."

Mateo drummed up the energy to hum. He felt the bed dip and Saul pull away. His heart sped up a little when he heard the bathroom water run.

A second later, Mateo felt the bed dip once more. He relaxed into Saul's cleaning ministration. A moment later and he felt Saul slide into bed behind him. The man kissed his neck again, curled his body around Mateo's, and held him.

With a smile on his lips, Mateo slipped into a restful slumber.

Hearing the ring of his phone, Saul peeled open one eyelid, then the second one. He gritted his teeth as he carefully eased away from his still sleeping mate. As much as Saul wanted to ignore it, he knew few outside members of his pod would call him, so it was probably important.

Awkwardly slinging an arm out, he managed to snag his slacks . . . and the belt that held his phone. He brought the device up and spotted Alpha Kaiser's name on the screen.

Damn.

Using a finger to swipe the screen, Saul accepted the call. "Hello." He kept his voice soft, hoping to allow his mate to continue sleeping.

"From your quiet tone, I'm guessing you're with your mate," Alpha Kaiser rumbled softly, also keeping his tone low. "Sorry to disturb you."

As his alpha had been speaking, Saul had begun carefully easing from the bed. He set his bare feet on the floor and rose to stand. Saul cast a longing look at his mate. Somehow the man appeared sexy and sweet even while snoring softly.

Turning away, Saul grunted in acknowledgement as he left the room. He closed the door most of the way, leaving it open a crack. Saul headed toward the small sofa and sat his naked butt on it.

"I've been alerted to some trouble that requires your special brand of expertise," Alpha Kaiser told him.

Rubbing his free hand over his face, Saul smirked. "You need me to go somewhere, throw my weight around, and act like an asshole."

Kaiser chuckled softly. "In a word, yep."

Saul quietly laughed, too. He didn't mind. After all, he was good at playing the sophisticated asshole lawyer. It was what he'd trained for.

"What's going on?" Saul asked, rising back to his feet and moving back toward the bedroom. "Where do I need to be?"

From the darkness filtering in from behind the window curtain Saul had closed before rejoining Mateo in bed, he knew the three-fifteen on the alarm clock meant AM.

Gods. I haven't even been holding my mate for five hours, and I'm being called away.

Saul grabbed his slacks and his shoes and headed back out of the room, closing the door silently that time.

"Ovram got an alert on his systems," Alpha Kaiser told him. "It seems Geoff has gotten himself into a spot of trouble."

As Saul listened, he pulled on his slacks before shoving his feet into his shoes.

"Geoff must have gotten into a bar fight. He's in lock-up."

Kaiser heaved a sigh. "I called Grisham first, but Geoff's not at his precinct, so it's not in his jurisdiction. He can't do much."

"Got it," Saul stated, grabbing Mateo's keys from a side table and heading out of the apartment. He locked the door behind him as he left and shoved them into his pocket. "Text me the precinct address, and I'll head down there." After just a second of hesitation, Saul added, "I'm grabbing my spare suit, then getting cleaned up here, so at least I'm already in the city."

"Truly, Saul. I am sorry about this." Alpha Kaiser sounded tired, which made sense, considering the hour. He sighed, adding, "I'm not sure what's up with Geoff. His temper's been getting the better of him of late."

"Jealous, I think," Saul guessed, going to his SUV. He used his own keys to open the vehicle, so he could reach in and grab the garment bag hanging in the back. He always carried a spare suit with him. "He wants his mate, just like all of us."

"Well, he won't find him or her by causing trouble," Kaiser grumbled. "Oh, I'm also putting out feelers for another lawyer who may want to join us here."

Alpha Kaiser was always careful with his words over the phone. Saul knew what he meant, and he wasn't offended. Getting another shifter to join their pod that was familiar with human laws would help free up some of his time for his mate.

"Thanks," Saul stated gratefully. "I'd appreciate that."

"Of course. Keep me posted."

The alpha disconnected the line, and Saul shoved his phone into his pocket before returning to Mateo's apartment, letting himself in with the borrowed keys.

Saul headed into the bathroom and used Mateo's toothbrush, hoping his mate wouldn't mind too much. He knew it was a damn intimate thing to do without permission. Then he showered, dried off, and dressed.

Within fifteen minutes, Saul was ready to leave, the address already waiting on his phone, compliments of Alpha Kaiser.

Hesitating in Mateo's bedroom doorway, Saul contemplated waking his sweet mate. The decision warred within him. He didn't want his mate to feel abandoned, but he didn't want to disturb what appeared to be a nice, deep restful sleep, either.

Saul decided to leave a note. After pressing a gentle kiss to his sleeping mate's temple, he left the room. Quietly, Saul searched the kitchen, coming up with a pen and blank recipe card. After a second of thought, he scrawled a short note, apologizing for needing to leave and hoping to catch him at the coffee shop for his break. Otherwise, he would call him that evening. Then Saul propped the card up on the coffee machine before heading out the door, leaving Mateo's keys behind.

Two hours later, Saul had secured Geoff's release. The large sea turtle shifter was normally a docile man. Like Alpha Kaiser had mentioned though, the black male had begun losing his temper and showing higher level of frustration.

Geoff worked as an engineer at *World of Aquatica*, keeping their elaborate system of tunnels and behind the scene machinery running. That way, shifters in the tanks could leave unnoticed by the human eye. That required a lot of fine-tuning and detail-oriented work. Geoff had always been patient and good at it.

Until recently.

Saul glanced at Geoff, who was sitting in the passenger seat. He still had a bit of dried blood at the corner of his lip, as well as some on his knuckles. His left eye was half-swollen shut. Not surprising, Geoff had refused to be seen by any medical professional for his injuries while in lock-up.

"After having Doc Anthony check you over, Alpha Kaiser wants to see you," Saul told the broader shifter. Seeing the grimace cross the large male's features, he quickly assured, "You know the alpha only wants to help." When that still didn't get a verbal response from the silent man, Saul went with the blunt approach. "Getting your ass beaten or beating someone up is no way to impress your mate when you run across him for the first time. Get your head out of your ass."

Sucking in a sharp breath, Geoff snapped his attention to Saul. A muscle ticked in his jaw even as he jerked a nod. "I know," he rumbled gruffly.

Saul left it at that. It wasn't his job to figure out the motives of the shifters in the pod.

Thank the gods for that.

CHAPTER SEVEN

"Your hottie is here again." Tina skipped into the room, excitement on her face. "And he's early."

"My hottie?" Mateo barely managed to swallow around the sudden lump in his throat. "Um, you sure?"

Why would Saul have come today? Doesn't leaving me in bed mean he isn't interested in more?

Mateo had tried so hard not to let disappointment flood him when he'd woken alone, but he hadn't managed it. Just like a chump, he'd swallowed Saul's lies—hook, line, and sinker. The man had used pretty words and a nice meal to get what he'd wanted—Mateo's ass—and then he was gone.

When Mateo had woken at seven-thirty, the sheets had even been cold. He'd curled up around the pillow Saul had used, breathing in the man's scent. If a few tears leaked out of his eyes, he would never admit that to anyone.

By the time Mateo had pulled himself together, he'd barely had enough time to take a quick shower before sprinting out the door, barely making it in time for work.

Tina's brows furrowed. "Yeah, he's here." Her smile dimmed as she touched his arm. "Is something wrong?"

"Uh, no. No, of course not," Mateo claimed. He hadn't told her about his date with Saul the prior evening. "Um, did he get his usual hot chai tea?"

Her smile back, Tina shook her head. "Nope. He got the iced chai like you took him yesterday."

Damn. Was that really just yesterday?

Mateo knew feeling heartache made the days seem like

weeks.

"Aaaaand," Tina continued, her voice taking on a sing-song quality. "He asked if you had your break yet." With a wink, Tina told him, "He wants you to join him."

"What?" Mateo would forever deny the squeak in his voice.

Laughing, Tina told him, "He even asked what your favorite coffee was so he could buy one for you."

Mateo shook his head in confusion.

Why would he do that?

Then a cold dread settled in his gut.

Maybe he plans to humiliate me in front of everyone.

Not happening.

Girding up his courage, Mateo told Tina, "Uh, well, will you send him back to the break room in twenty minutes, then?" That would hopefully give him time to shore up his resolve against the man's uber sexiness. "That's when Marshal told me to take my break."

Tina nodded. "Okay." With a grin, she sauntered back toward the front.

All too soon, Mateo's break time arrived.

Mateo dried his hands and headed into the breakroom. Stepping inside, he froze just inside the door, realizing Saul was already there. The tall man was relaxing on one of the small sofas, a tablet in his hand, and looking good enough to eat in designer jeans and a short-sleeved polo shirt.

When Saul lifted his attention from his tablet and focused on him, his lips curving in a heart-stopping smile, Mateo felt his mouth go dry. His heart skipped a beat in his chest. For an instant, Mateo forgot all about the pain of waking up alone to an empty bed and an empty apartment. He'd lain there for several minutes listening for any hint that the man might have just gotten up to go to the bathroom or something.

That hadn't been the case.

Just that fast, Mateo's pleasure at seeing Saul morphed into frustration with a hint of bitterness. He clenched his jaw for a second while swallowing hard. Staring to the left of Saul's head, Mateo managed to find his tongue.

"What are you doing here?"

Mateo wanted to pat himself on the back for keeping his tone nice and even, but that would have been weird.

"I told you I was going to try to join you for your break," Saul claimed, setting his tablet on the nearby table, which already held two mugs. When Mateo didn't respond, wondering when Saul had told him that, Saul rose while continuing, "In my note. The one I left you."

"A note?" Mateo barely managed to whisper the words. *Saul left me a note?*

With a sigh, Saul crossed the room, saying, "I gather you didn't see it, though. I left it by the coffee pot." His smile turned strained as he told him, "You work at a coffee shop. I figured you'd have some first thing. Most coffee drinkers do." Stopping before Mateo, Saul murmured, "I've heard it's been called the morning nectar of the gods or some such bullshit."

Unable to help himself, Mateo pressed close to Saul, resting his hands on his hips. "You weren't there when I woke up." He couldn't help how accusatory he sounded. "I ended up running late. I didn't use my coffee pot. I got a cup here."

"I'm so sorry, baby," Saul murmured into his ear, nuzzling his chin against his temple. "My boss called me a little after three this morning. Had to go to work."

Mateo tipped his chin up, staring up at Saul with furrowed brows. "He expected you to work at three in the morning?" When Saul began to nod, Mateo couldn't help but ask, "Does that happen often?"

Saul grimaced. "A bit more often than I'd like these days." His lips curved into a wry smile. "You know how I said that I'm Kaiser Roush's sole lawyer?" When Mateo nodded, Saul told him, "Well, that's going to change." Lifting a hand, he traced his fingers along Mateo's jaw. "That way, I'll have more time to spend with you."

A warm glow filled Mateo's stomach. "Really?" he whispered. "You'd take less work for me?"

"Absolutely," Saul declared, his expression serious. "You're far more important than any work."

As Saul settled his mouth over Mateo, and he welcomed his lover's kiss, all he could think was, "Wow."

Saul had spent every evening with Mateo, rebuilding the trust his thoughtlessness had broken. He'd learned that his sweet mate had self-esteem issues. His wonderful human still seemed to be having a hell of a time accepting the fact that Saul wanted him, and only him.

I hope revealing paranormals helps him understand that he's everything to me.

And hopefully, he doesn't wonder if I'm stuck with him because of Fate.

While, from a certain point of view, that could be considered true, Saul had never heard of a paranormal feeling that way. From the time a paranormal learned about having a perfect fated mate out there, someone made just for them, they were always on the search for that person. Meeting them, bonding with them, twining their life threads, was a gift — the fulfillment of a promise that they would no longer walk the world alone.

Tuesday had finally arrived, and Saul looked forward to taking Mateo on the promised boat ride. He drove them north, past *World of Aquatica*, to their shifter pod's private marina. As he drove past the place most of his pod-mates worked, Saul pointed at it.

"Have you ever been there?" Saul asked curiously.

Mateo nodded. "Once, years ago when it first opened."

With a sad chuckle, he admitted, "My family went as a huge group on one of the family day discounts."

Saul nodded, understanding how those memories would be bittersweet for his mate. "Have you heard from Emilio much?"

He didn't mention it, but he'd been in contact with a paranormal child custody lawyer — Clive. The vampire had taken the information Ovram had dug up on Mateo's family. If he needed to, he could call Clive and the male would help.

"Yeah," Mateo replied with a nod. "He calls every few days, during the day when he's at school." With a grimace, Mateo admitted, "That way, his parents don't find out. He memorized my number, and I explained how to delete the record of the call from the device afterward."

"I'm sorry you have to skulk around to talk to your nephew." Saul reached out and gave Mateo's hand a reassuring squeeze.

Saul would have tried to knock some sense into Santiago's head if he thought it would do any good, but bigots normally didn't change without some serious impetus.

Mateo shrugged. Flipping his hand, he threaded their fingers together and squeezed Saul's. His smile relaxed a bit as he murmured, "Can't control anyone but yourself."

Nodding in acknowledgement, Saul took the turn to their marina. "This is a little steep, but it's perfectly safe," he assured.

Then Saul guided the SUV around the bend, revealing not only a stunning view of the ocean and marina, but a drop off, as well.

Yanking his hand away, Mateo gasped. "Two hands on the wheel, please." At the same time, his sweet human grabbed the *oh shit* handle.

Saul smiled but did as his mate bid. He'd heard that was the reaction from others the first time their mates took them to the marina. The way down could definitely be considered intimidating.

Once Saul reached the bottom and parked in a small parking lot, he shut off the SUV. He rested his palm on Mateo's leg and gave it a few rhythmic squeezes. Slowly, the tension beneath his fingers eased and Mateo's breathing relaxed.

"Wow," Mateo mumbled, his cheeks taking on just a hint of pink. "Didn't expect that."

"This is a private marina, owned by Kaiser and William, so they don't adhere to certain safety rules like a public one would."

Mateo nodded. "Right."

"Come on," Saul encouraged, eager to not only share the day with Mateo, but to share his nature with him, too. "Let's get out there. The day is clear and the ocean is calling."

"Okay."

Saul exited the vehicle, closing the door behind him. He opened the back hatch and slung two straps over his shoulders—one to a duffel holding his brand-new inflatable banana and the second holding spare clothes and a soft-sided cooler with drinks. "Do you mind carrying the basket of food?"

"Sure." Mateo grabbed it.

After closing the door, Saul grabbed Mateo's free hand and led the way toward the marina. He didn't get out on the boats very often, and he looked forward to sharing it with his mate. Normally, Saul only headed into the water in his lion's mane jellyfish form.

Hope Mateo doesn't freak out when I show him.

At least he won't be able to run away.

Saul had tucked some smelling salts in the bag he carried, just in case Mateo fainted. He'd heard that was a thing some humans ended up doing.

"Wow," Mateo whispered, his head swiveling this way

and that. "That yacht is huge." He glanced toward Saul in surprise. "Are we taking that out? How's it even get in here? I can't imagine the water'd be deep enough."

"No, we're not taking that out," Saul told him, hoping his mate wasn't disappointed. "And Kaiser and William dug a trench for it, that way it could dock here."

The pair were massive squid shifters — a colossal and giant squid respectively — and had easily used their thick tentacles to move the sand and dirt.

"Wow." Mateo sounded impressed even as he shook his head. "So, what are we taking?"

Mateo looked over the other crafts — a couple of smaller yachts, a few sail boats, a couple of fishing trawlers, and in the back . . . a high-end speedboat.

"That one," Saul claimed, using his chin to indicate the large, speedy craft.

Shuffling a few steps in obvious excitement, Mateo's face lit up with glee. "Really?"

There was even a squeak in his mate's voice, but Saul didn't comment on it.

"*Really,*" Saul confirmed, pleasure filling him that Mateo liked his choice. "Let's go have some fun."

Saul loved the huge smile on Mateo's face as he helped his mate into the boat. They stowed their gear before Saul untied the mooring lines. With a turn of the key, the craft's six four-hundred-fifty horse-powered engines roared to life.

Mateo grasped the railing as well as a handle near his seat, but his wide excited grin told Saul that his mate wasn't worried. In fact, his lover practically vibrated in his seat.

Carefully, keeping them slow, Saul maneuvered them away from the marina and toward deeper water. When they were farther out, he flashed his own grin Mateo's way as he hollered, "Hang on!" Then Saul revved the engines, and they shot forward across the waves.

Hearing Mateo's squeal, Saul glanced his way in concern. He grinned again, seeing the joy written all over his mate's face. Keeping half his attention on the horizon so they wouldn't get close to hitting anything, Saul found the rest of his focus on Mateo's obvious pleasure.

His mate was loving it.

After a short while, Saul slowed them and patted his lap. "Come here, Mateo." Seeing his mate's questioning look, he told him, "Come learn to drive."

Mateo's look of uncertainty was quickly overtaken by an expression of excitement. He took Saul's offered hand and settled on his thigh, cuddling into his chest. Pleasure filled Saul, and he wrapped his arm securely around Mateo's waist as he shifted his feet to brace them better.

Then Saul walked Mateo through driving the boat.

Within seconds, they were once again cruising across the waves. He listened to his mate's squeals of glee, his gut and heart churning with unfamiliar sensations. Saul loved pleasing his mate, and he could see them doing this damn near every week.

More often, if I can convince my mate to give up his job and move in with me.

Pushing those thoughts to the back of his mind, Saul enjoyed the moment.

After a while, Saul urged Mateo to guide the boat closer to shore. "Ready to try out the banana tug tube?" he asked upon seeing Mateo's questioning look.

"Yeah," Mateo quickly agreed.

Saul eased out from under Mateo, allowing his mate to watch out for things while he prepped the inflatable. The thing ended up taking several minutes to inflate, even with the electric pump. While it did that, Saul sorted out the rope.

Once everything was ready, Saul helped Mateo into a wetsuit and a life jacket. The last thing he wanted was to endanger his mate. Saul figured someday, it might not be necessary, but today wasn't that day.

After I've introduced him to my jellyfish, so he knows I'd never hurt him and will always keep him safe in deep water.

Then Saul held the banana steady as Mateo climbed aboard.

Keeping the engines low to start, Saul started them moving, keeping a sharp eye on the love of his life being tugged behind him.

Hearing Mateo's hollers to go faster, Saul laughed and complied.

CHAPTER EIGHT

Mateo couldn't believe Saul had allowed him to drive the boat. The thing was . . . massive and powerful and so far out of his league. The damn thing had six engines, and he'd been afraid to see how fast he was going.

He couldn't imagine the price tag on the craft.

Not only that, but Saul had bought the banana tube, just as he'd promised. Mateo never would have imagined the slender man getting on it. Except, he had. Saul had insisted that he get to try it, so he'd left Mateo on the boat — all by himself — to pull him through the waves.

Just wow!

After finishing with the banana tube, Saul'd driven them to a secluded cove. He'd put down the anchor and pulled out a picnic basket as well as a cooler from the duffel bag. From within, Saul revealed a large charcutier selection — meats, cheeses, fruits, and crackers of a variety of kinds and flavors. He'd pulled out a bottle of champagne along with a couple of flutes.

Saul popped the cork and filled the flutes. With a smile, he handed one to Mateo.

"Thanks." Mateo took the glass of light-colored, bubbly liquid, admitting, "I've never had champagne before."

"If you don't like it, I have other options," Saul assured him, settling on a seat cushion next to him. He pressed a kiss to Mateo's lips before relaxing against the back and taking a sip. Then he grabbed a small plastic plate and began filling it with food. "Can I prepare you a plate? Is there anything you don't like?"

Mateo chuckled, feeling relaxed and a little tired from all the activity. "Sure, and I'll try anything."

"Again, if you don't like it, don't eat it," Saul told him, sliding a plate full of items toward him. After taking a sip of champagne, he placed the glass in a grooved slot obviously meant to hold stemware. As he began dishing up more food on a second plate, Saul grinned at him. "I'm not going to ask if you enjoyed yourself, because I know you did. I hope we can do this together often."

"Yeah," Mateo agreed. "I'd like that." Then Mateo took a sip of the champagne. He hummed, finding the flavor a little more bitter than he'd anticipated, but he didn't mind it. "Not bad."

Saul chuckled.

Mateo smiled at the man who'd slept in his bed every evening for the last four days, showing him the greatest pleasures imaginable. His prick began thickening just thinking about their evenings together, and he was glad he was no longer wearing the wetsuit. Doing his best to push those stimulating thoughts from his mind, Mateo focused on his food.

As Mateo popped the cracker topped with prosciutto and some kind of spicy cheese into his mouth, Saul used his flute to point toward sea. Following where his lover indicated — *wow, I actually have a lover* — he spotted a blast of water rise into the air. A second later, the unmistakable topline of a whale appeared above the water less than a hundred yards from them.

"Oh, wow." Mateo grinned. "I didn't think it was the right time of year for whale watching."

The whale blew again before rolling in the water, for all the world looking as if it was showing off for them.

"It's really not," Saul confirmed. "That's Ezekiel. His friends call him Zeke."

Confused, Mateo glanced Saul's way. The man appeared completely serious. "Uh, Ezekiel? Zeke?" He chuckled, grabbing a large green olive. "What do you mean?" With a shake of his head, Mateo pointed at it before popping the olive into his mouth. "It's a humpback whale, which is really cool, by the way, but why call it Ezekiel or Zeke?" Then, around his mouthful of food, Mateo muttered, "Oh, is it one that's got a tracker on it? Do you know someone in the industry that's keeping tabs on humpbacks?"

Mateo thought that would be an amazing industry to be in—dedicated to the conservation of endangered marine animals.

"Ah, no." Saul shook his head. "Nothing like that." He let out a quiet scoff before his smile turned wry. "I have something sort of crazy to explain, and I was hoping that seeing Ezekiel would help ease you into it." Getting up, Saul headed toward a live-well. "I had a friend stow these this morning before we got to the marina," he revealed, opening the lid. "Yeah, Zeke will like these."

To Mateo's surprise, Saul reached in and pulled out a large salmon, holding it firmly by the tail.

"Wow, how'd you catch that?" Mateo couldn't imagine how Saul managed to move fast enough to snag a salmon by the tail.

Saul winked at him and carried it over to him. "I'm faster than I look," he told him before banging on the side of the boat. "Now, just watch."

Mateo looked from Saul to the fish in confusion, which was wriggling and flopping, clearly trying to get free. Saul held fast, though, even as he held it over the side of the boat. Movement toward sea caught Mateo's eye, and he gasped.

The whale was moving toward them steadily.

Instinctively, Mateo tensed, readying to move away.

"Just relax," Saul urged, rubbing his back. "You're completely safe."

Mateo didn't relax, but he did stay still.

The whale came up alongside their boat. Lifting its front out of the water, it opened its mouth. Saul swung the fish and released it, and just like a dolphin in a show, the humpback caught the fish in its mouth before sinking beneath the waves.

Barking a laugh, Mateo shook his head in amazement. "Did I really see what I just saw?" he squeaked, glancing from the whale that appeared to be circling back toward them and Saul. "Did you just feed a whale?"

"Yep," Saul replied with a smile. He reached a hand out and pointed. "Zeke'll let you pet him, if you want."

Full of wonder, Mateo couldn't resist that offer. "O-Okay," he stuttered, still feeling a smidge of trepidation.

"Zeke won't hurt you, Mateo," Saul assured as the huge whale came close to the boat again. "I promise."

As if to confirm his words, the big animal issued some kind of lowing bellow while floating beside them. Mateo assumed it would sound like whale song if he were under water. With his heart hammering in his chest, Mateo followed Saul's guidance and skimmed his palm over the huge animal's dark-gray hide.

"Wow." Mateo just couldn't stop saying that. "I-I'm touching a whale."

"Ezekiel's not just a whale," Saul countered with a smile. He focused on the beast in the water. "Want another salmon? Malcolm put two more in there for you. I appreciate you doing this for me."

The whale—Ezekiel—actually bobbed its head in the water in a sort of nod.

Saul rose to his feet and headed back to the live-well.

Mateo watched as his lover stuck in his arms and came back with a fish in each hand. "How the hell?" he whispered, totally shocked.

Staring in a mixture of disbelief and wonder, Mateo watched Saul as he fed Ezekiel both fish. The whale didn't move on after that, as if happy as could be to hang out with them. Mateo even thought he noticed a hint of concern in the beast's huge gray eye as it looked up at him.

"What the hell is going on?" Mateo whispered.

Settling back in his seat, Saul wrapped his arm around Mateo's shoulders. "So, as I said, Ezekiel is not simply a whale. He's a paranormal being known as a shifter." His gaze remained steady upon him when he told him, "Ezekiel also has a human form, but he's sentient as his whale, too."

Mateo couldn't help but just stare, trying to get what he'd just heard to actually make sense.

Paranormal. Shifter. Sentient as a whale.

Nope. Not computing.

"What?" Mateo shook his head once before glancing at the food and drink. "D-Did you slip me something?"

Saul shook his head, his smile turning a mixture of fond and worried. "No, I didn't slip you anything. This is all real." His brows furrowed a little as he appeared thoughtful. Then he indicated the live-well. "The reason I had no trouble catching the salmon is because I share my spirit with a jellyfish. A lion's mane jellyfish, to be exact. One of the largest species." Saul sounded damn proud of that fact. "I can turn my fingers into a few of my tentacles, so it was easy to catch the salmon, then turn my tentacles back into fingers while holding the fish." With a shrug, Saul claimed, "I just did it out of your sight so I didn't freak you out."

Mateo shook his head again, glancing at Saul's hands. Confusion blanketed his mind as he imagined long, jellyfish tentacles coming out of lover's fingers. He couldn't make the man's words compute.

"I-I-I . . ." Mateo had no idea what to say.

Saul sighed. "They do say that seeing is believing, so I'll

show you. Try not to freak out now, okay?"

A few seconds later, Mateo watched as Saul held up his hand and his fingers . . . changed.

Mateo didn't freak out. No, instead, his eyes rolled to the back of his head, and he fainted.

"I heard from Ezekiel that your mate took the whole paranormal reveal well, all things considered."

Saul smiled upon hearing Beta William's amused voice come through the speaker of his SUV. "All things considered," he confirmed with a chuckle.

Saul wasn't surprised that Ezekiel had passed on a report to the beta of their pod. Saul had been too busy fucking his mate over every surface of the jetboat, then his suite. Saul hadn't been able to help himself.

Once Saul had explained everything paranormal and shifter related to Mateo—his mate had asked a million questions and had needed to be reassured, twice, that Saul didn't consider himself *stuck* with Mateo—his mate had agreed to move in with him. His human was even putting in his two-week notice today. Saul was on his way to the coffee shop to pick him up so they could go celebrate . . . then start packing up his apartment.

"I'm glad I brought those smelling salts like you recommended," Saul told William. "Better than splashing salt water on his face."

"Kinder and gentler, too," William teased. "So when's he moving in?"

"Tomorrow after work," Saul stated happily, so very pleased that his mate would finally be in his own space. "We're celebrating and packing tonight. Think a few of the guys will help me lift heavy objects tomorrow?"

William chuckled. "Of course. I'll make certain Geoff is

there, too." He sobered a little as he told him, "The exercise will be a good stress reliever for him."

"Yeah." Saul had heard Geoff had gotten into another fight, but because it was with a well-known troublemaker, everyone had considered it the human's fault. "He needs someone to keep an eye on him. How's he in animal form?" he asked curiously.

With a sigh, William explained, "His animal seems fine. He still enjoys his favorite sunning rock. It's just his human half that's annoyed, impatient, and testy." The beta huffed a growl before saying, "I've put eyes on him for anytime he leaves *World of Aquatica,* though, so don't worry about it."

Saul nodded as he found a parking spot near the coffee shop. "I'm here," he told his beta. "Give me a sec to switch to my phone." After doing just that, Saul slid a speaking device over his ear and attached his phone to his belt. He headed toward the coffee shop, his long legs eating up the ground quickly. "I'll let you know how much stuff will need to be moved and how much help we'll need."

That was one nice thing about being in a shifter pod—lots of people who could move heavy objects and plenty of arms to do it.

"Good. Oh, also, did you need to switch condos?" William asked. "I know you're in a two-bedroom right now, and you use one as your office. Do you need a three-bedroom?"

Considering that with a hum, Saul entered the coffee shop. He knew his mate loved making craft items out of shells. A third bedroom or a suite with two-bedrooms and an office or den would give Mateo plenty of space to do it. Saul really liked that idea.

"I think that may be a good idea," Saul told William. "But I'd like Mateo to have a chance to decide on the space. Can you shoot me a list of available places?" Recalling how much Mateo enjoyed watching the sea, Saul asked, "Are any of the seaside cottages available?"

"Not currently," William told him, disappointing Saul. Then his beta offered, "But it'd be damn easy to get something built. Then it could even be to your specifications."

Saul grinned. "I like that idea."

William laughed, saying, "I thought you might. I'll start looking at plots and —"

"Hold up, William," Saul murmured softly, his gaze falling on a young man he recognized. "Can I call you back?"

"Sure. Problem?" His beta obviously recognized the concern in his voice.

"Maybe. Talk soon." Saul disconnected the line and headed toward the gangly teenager standing off to the side of the line. The young Hispanic male was looking around the place, appearing uncertain. Keeping his voice soft, Saul asked, "Emilio?"

Emilio spun to face him. His deep brown eyes were the same shade as Mateo's, and he shared the same wide forehead and cheekbones. His expression appeared fearful, and his scent stank of it enough to tease Saul's senses even over the coffee smell.

Staring up at him, Emilio whispered, "You're Mateo's boyfriend."

Saul nodded. "Yeah." Offering Emilio a reassuring smile, he told him, "Although, I prefer the term partner." Feeling beyond pleased, Saul added, "He is moving in with me tomorrow, after all."

To Saul's surprise, Emilio's shoulders sagged and he wrapped his arms around his torso. His body language screamed disappointment. His words revealed even more.

"Oh," Emilio whispered, shuddering out a breath. "Guess the idea of moving in with him is out."

Saul really didn't like the way that sounded and knew he needed to get the boy alone. Glancing around, he spotted Tina behind the counter. She was sending concerned looks his way. Saul smiled at her even as he rested a hand on Emilio's shoulder, doing his best to ignore the way the human tensed.

"Mateo's nephew and I are going to wait for my man in the breakroom," Saul told Tina. "He's going on break in, what?" He glanced at the clock before focusing on her again. "Ten minutes?"

Over the last few days, Saul had become pretty good at arriving shortly before Mateo went on break.

Tina smiled brightly at him. "Sure thing, Mateo's hottie. I'll let him know you and" — she paused, staring at Emilio, so Saul supplied a name and she nodded, continuing — "you and Emilio are here."

"Thanks, Tina." Saul had always liked the vibrant young woman. "Come on, Emilio."

As soon as they made it to the breakroom, Emilio eased away from Saul, but Saul wasn't surprised. "So," Saul began, offering the teenager a kind smile. "Want anything from the vending machine?" He indicated said machine.

Emilio hesitated before shaking his head. "No, thanks." His dark brows were furrowed. "How do you know me?"

"Saw you talking to Mateo at the restaurant Friday night," Saul answered truthfully. "Mateo's talked about his family. About you." Seeing Emilio begin to pale, Saul quickly stated, "He thinks very highly of you." When Emilio blushed, ducking his head but not saying anything, Saul asked, "Did your father find out you're gay and kick you out? Or did you run away?"

As Saul asked the questions, he studied the teenager's facial tics. He knew even before Emilio replied what the answer would be, and he had to bank the rage he felt on the youngster's behalf.

"K-Kicked me out," Emilio mumbled, looking at the floor. "F-Found my p-porn."

"Nosy father," Saul stated idly as he pulled out his phone. "Hey, William," he greeted when the beta picked up. "I'm going to need that three-bedroom immediately, after all. Mateo and I will be joined by Mateo's nephew, Emilio."

"Damn, okay. This'll make things . . . interesting for a while." William chuckled. "I'll round up some guys to get things set up for you."

"I appreciate it," Saul told his pod's second-in-command. He knew William knew all about Emilio, considering their people had been looking into Mateo's family. "I'm not sure how long we'll be, but I'll text you more later." He figured William would make certain everyone was aware of what was up. Saul couldn't remember the last time their pod had had an un-knowing human—a human who didn't know who and what they were or even that paranormals existed—living within their midst, but Saul knew they would make it work. "Talk to you soon."

"Y-You'd let me live with you?" Emilio gaped at him, his eyes wide. "J-Just like that?"

Saul nodded. "Of course." Reaching out, he squeezed the young human's shoulder again before releasing him. "Just like that." Seeing that Emilio still didn't appear convinced, Saul sighed and told him, "Emilio, I know you don't know me, but you're Mateo's nephew. He loves you. I love Mateo." Saul shrugged. "It's as simple as that. Making certain you're taken care of will make Mateo happy, which will make me happy."

It was the paranormal way of mates, not that Saul could explain that to Emilio.

"Y-You love me?"

Turning, Saul spotted Mateo standing in the doorway. He smiled. "Yeah, baby. I love you."

After a glance between them, Mateo refocused on Saul. "A-And Emilio can live with us?" He looked worried. "That'll be allowed?"

Saul knew what Mateo was referring to—the fact that Emilio didn't know about shifters. With a smile, he told his mate, "Mateo, Emilio is your family. That means he's my family," Saul stated gravely, staring deep into his mate's worried brown eyes. "My people take good care of our family."

Seconds later, Saul found his arms full of a very grateful Mateo. "I love you, too, Saul," his mate whispered before he tilted his head up, offering a kiss Saul was only too happy to take. He hugged his mate tightly to him for a much-too-brief a time before Mateo was pulling away, but he understood why.

In the next instant, Mateo wrapped Emilio in his arms. "You're coming home with us," his mate declared with a smile. "We'll take care of everything."

Emilio glanced between them, worriedly nibbling his bottom lip, and Saul knew exactly where the teenager had learned the move. "Are you sure?" he whispered uncertainly. He turned a worried gaze on Saul. "Y-You don't m-mind me m-moving in with y-you guys?"

Saul patted Emilio on the shoulder lightly. "I don't mind, Emilio. You're family," he reiterated. "We'll help you decide where you want to go and what you want to do." With a growl, Saul added, "We'd *never* allow our family to be homeless just because they're different."

When Emilio's eyes lit with relief, his body sagging against Mateo's, Saul knew he'd made the right decision. Sure, taking in a human teenager would turn his life upside-down, but it would be worth it. After all, anything was worth making Mateo happy.

"Hey, Mateo." An older human appeared in the doorway, his expression grave. "Sorry for eavesdropping, but I heard what happened." He offered a commiserating smile as he stated, "Why don't you take the rest of the day off. Looks like you have more important things to deal with."

"You sure, Marshal?" Mateo asked, sounding amazed.

Marshal nodded. "Yeah. See you tomorrow." With a half-wave and nod, he began allowing the breakroom door close behind him. "Take care, guys."

"Damn, he's an amazing boss," Mateo whispered, shaking his head in obvious surprise.

Saul had to agree. Marshal was one of the good ones.

Hmmm . . . wonder if he's single. Maybe he's Geoff's type.

Pushing the errant thought from his mind, Saul pecked a kiss to Mateo's temple. "Come on, guys," he encouraged. "We have stuff to pack and move."

With his arm around Mateo's waist and Mateo's arm around Emilio's shoulders, Saul led his new little family out of the coffee shop. He guided them toward his SUV, more than happy to accept any kind of chaos the situation would bring. With his pod backing him, Saul knew they could handle it.

ABOUT THE AUTHOR

Charlie started writing fantasy when she was eight, and after stumbling onto her first erotic romance at age nineteen, she realized her true calling. She now focuses on writing gay erotic romance, normally of the paranormal variety, with heroes of all kinds. With the help and support of her husband, Charlie finally fulfilled one of her life-long goals . . . move to acreage with her horses. You can often find her curled up with her laptop and a cup of tea or glass of wine, creating her next adventure. Charlie enjoys exploring the mountains of her new Oregon home on horseback, 4-wheeler, or motorcycle.

She can be reached at ch.richards2010@yahoo.com

Or visit her at www.charlie-richards.com.

www.ingramcontent.com/pod-product-compliance
Lightning Source LLC
Chambersburg PA
CBHW070538130626

46555CB00003B/1478